AN ANGEL
NOT PERCEIVED

iii

AN ANGEL NOT PERCEIVED

Leaving the Realms of Heaven and Descending to Earth

Dr. Robert J. Newton

Beyond the Bounds of Earth Publishing
Entertainment and Education | Great Motivational Talks

ISBN: 978-0-9961371-7-1

Also available on Kindle

Dr. Robert J. Newton
561 S. 14th St.
Grover Beach, California 93433
www.drrobertnewton.com

Dr. Robert J. Newton, J.D., N.D.,
3rd Degree Kriya Kundalini Master,
3rd Degree Ascelpiad

Ordering Information:
Quantity sales. Special discounts are available on quantity purchases by corporations, associations, and others. For details, contact the publisher at the address above.

Printed in the United States of America
First Edition: 10 9 8 7 6 5 4 3 2 1

Dedication

THIS BOOK IS dedicated to my wife of 38 years, Charlette Newton Smith, who re-ascended to the realms of heaven in June 2013. She was my first real love, first and third wife, my best friend, and teacher supreme. Her teaching and support created the impetus for me to write about what other writers appear to gloss over!

Dr. Robert J. Newton

*An Angel is not a little being with
wings, it represents symbolically, the next
stage of the evolution of Humankind...our
capacity to dream, to travel, to activate the
multidimensions of our consciousness...*

~ Professor/Global Ambassador Francis L. Kaya

Table of Contents

Preface

EVEN AS A prolific author, I never considered I would ever write a book about an Angel or Angels. At one time, I considered the talk about Angels to be idle babble. Yet over time, I began to study about the Seraphim's—the high Angels—including the Arc Angel Michael and later, the Arc Angel Metatron, both of whom are at the top of the "Tree of Life," from the Kabbalah. I have also assiduously studied the *72 Names of God*, from Exodus 14:19-21 of the *Torah*, and the Ninth Name of God is *Hey Zayin Yod*, which means invoking Angels. I guess all of these, plowed furrows in my head, into which fell seeds, that germinated and grew themselves into beautiful forms that changed my perspective of things.

My knowledge of Angels was certainly expanded by studying the *72 Angels of God*, from the Kabbalah. I would strongly recommend the study of these things, to all people of all persuasions!

Acknowledgements

MANY THANKS TO my editor and writing coach, Anna Weber of Voices in Print Publishing. She tweaks the pages of my books and adds the frosting on them, which makes it taste much better!

AN ANGEL NOT PERCEIVED

CHAPTER ONE

COMING BACK TO EARTH FROM THE LOFTY PERCH OF HEAVEN

ONCE IN A great while, people can lift the veil between the various dimensions in the Universe and remember from whence they came before incarnating on Earth. Something similar to this occurs at the time of *Dia De Los Muertos* and Halloween, when—around October 30th and 31st—the veil is at its thinnest of all the days of the year, because the space between the Earth dimension and the realms of the heavens, is considerably less.

At this time, it is much easier to contact those who left Earth...to feel their presence, and to communicate with them telepathically... sometimes actually in person. Angels can make us aware of many things because of the broader perspective of things from the heavens, and because of the higher dimensions they inhabit. They also communicate with us, although very few people are aware of this occurring. Even if they are aware, they are more naturally terrified and/or baffled by this type of heavenly communication!

Much rarer than this communication, however, is when someone leaves the high realms of Heaven and descends to Earth, reincarnating again...in a supreme sacrifice! Life in the fourth, fifth, sixth, seventh, eighth and ninth dimensional realms of Heaven, is immeasurably easier to live and much more enjoyable. This is because the higher you ascend into an elevated dimension, the more things exist in a state of light and energy, due to a higher distribution of atomic geometries, as per Valery P. Kondratov's, *Geometry of a Uniform Field*. Conditions like sickness and disease are unknown, because you live within—and are aware that everything is—energy...and matter is relegated to the myth from whence it came! Sickness and death simply do not exist in these higher dimensions!

Ah! The awareness within the discoveries of Quantum Physics and Quantum Mechanics and knowing there is much less resistance and friction at work against the manifestation of things. A person who exists in higher dimensions can move their body, which we now know is comprised more of light rather than dense matter...through their thoughts and at the speed of light. It is this ease of teleportation that allows people to easily communicate with those of us existing on the third dimension of Earth!

Going to the fourth dimension, the first level of heaven, is a common occurrence; when most people pass on, they are not prepared to live in the fifth and higher dimensions. This inability is due to a lack of good works performed and being limited by a general lack of understanding about the infinite possibilities that have been bestowed upon us by our benevolent Creator/God. The dimension a person inhabits is dependent upon their works to help other people on Earth and their spiritual practices, including deep levels of mediation and the recitation of prayers, mantras and rosaries they perform! It is really less important, to our position in the heavens, whether someone has been "saved" by Jesus or any of the many other Masters and Sons of God who came to Earth such as Buddha, Krishna, Rama, Osiris, Thoth, and St. Germaine, but not limited thereto!

All of this digression is necessary just to appreciate when an Angel agrees to leave the comfort of the very highest levels of Heaven. When the exalted Enoch ascended into the heavens, in a ball of light, as described in *The Book of Enoch,* we find a description of Enoch going through succeeding higher dimensions of heaven, until he arrived at his destination of "The Tree of Life," in the Tenth Heaven, just above the abode of the high Angels of God, in the Ninth Paradise, which is the Ninth Heaven, talked about in *The Book of Enoch*, as the Ninth Dimension.

Ann was just such an Angel, who was from the Ninth Paradise, and agreed to take on the mission to uplift and teach the people Earth so we can unlock our true divine potential, as per *Aleph Kaf Aleph*...the Seventh "Name of God" from Exodus in the Torah, which means to restore things to their perfect state. Without coincidence, the Seventh Angel of God, Achaiah, also known as the Angel of patience, is related to *Aleph Kaf Aleph*, and known for great patience and taking on difficult tasks. Particularly important, given the nature and scope of Ann's task would require the Angel's assistance and guidance.

Although Ann could have come back to Earth as a Master Teacher such as Jesus, Buddha, Krishna, Satchi Sai Baba, Sri Aurobindo, Amachi, Kwan Yuen, Mataji, or Babaji Nagaraj, she agreed to abide by the decision of "The Council of The White Brotherhood." This group is one of the ruling forces in the highest realms of Heaven, and subject to our Creator/God. Ann could have walked into someone else's body, in the manner described in Ruth Montgomery's book, *Stranger's Among Us,* where someone ready to leave Earth allows a discarnate soul the right to come into and inhabit their body, Yet she agreed to reincarnate as a woman of humble means and to be born through the womb of a mother, instead of the soul exchange process of a walk-in. This is exactly how Master Satchi Sai Baba comes back to Earth, through the womb, even though he is a master of space and time and can teleport into any dimension or realm he desires. This is a concept well known in India but few people outside of that country know or understand it!

Anyway, it occurred that Ann found a fetus in a mother of humble means on Earth, who had not been claimed by another soul waiting to reincarnate to Earth. Likewise, the family she would incarnate into was of common and simple origins. In this specific case, having a mother of humble means also came with genetic problems carried by the mother in her DNA. Unfortunately, these problems were not set in stone and could have been circumvented with epigenetic practices and the changing of a person's thoughts and emotions, which affect DNA.

Epigenetics utilizes health protocols to make a change in DNA. Although it is still believed once you have your DNA you are stuck with it for life, recent research shows that not only certain health practices can change DNA, but prayer, mantra, rosary and chanting can also affect and change it. And in fact, a person's emotions can improve DNA or further damage it.

The problem with Ann's situation was that in 1949 virtually no one knew what epigenetics was and only Christian Scientist's, through their textbook, *Science and Health with Key to the Scriptures*, by Mary Baker Eddy, even considered how thoughts and emotions created sickness, disease and lack in our lives. Thus, Ann knew; she was aware she would be born with genetic complications involving her teeth, liver, heart, pancreas, adrenals and uterus! Compounding things further, her mother smoked and drank alcoholic beverages, which of course today we know can cause birth defects by damaging a person's DNA and genes. Ann's life would be rife with health challenges...this she knew as a certitude!

With many caveats, which even an Angel cannot circumvent by being incarnated here through a womb, Ann was born a Leo, on August 11, 1949. The genetic defects mentioned above were not apparent when Ann was a baby, although she was born slightly premature and was of a weight of barely more than five pounds. As a child, Ann was rather sickly and not highly infused with energy or vibrancy! Nevertheless, being an Angel at her essence, Ann knew how to deal with the problems and did so in state of silence and tranquility, without much fuss or copious amounts of crying, as almost all babies in a similar situation would do!

One thing which Ann did not like was the cold, windy winters and the hot, humid summers of the Chicago area where she was born. Being the first baby and child in her family meant she got a lot of attention from her parents, Celestial and Edwin, and from relatives and her parent's friends. When a second child came later, followed by two others, Ann was no longer the center of attention in the household. However, being of Angelic origins, such things were not important to her, since Angel's always put other people before themselves. Hence, through Angelic behaviors not representing jealousy or resentment, Anne was already leaving an imprint, known as a morphic field (thought form) on Earth—in contradistinction to the normal reaction of first-born children who generally react negatively to new family additions!

The second and third children, both sisters, exhibited no genetic defects—either at birth or later. However, the fourth child, a boy named Gerome, manifested a genetic defect of Diabetes, and by five years old had to take a daily insulin shot. The disease, a constant burden, subsequently left him with very little joy or meaning in his life. Additionally, Gerome experienced huge mood swings due to fluctuations in his blood sugar levels, causing fits of rage and anger. This obviously left a strong impression on Ann and her sisters since they were in fear of what might result from Gerome's temper tantrums. In fact, it was with some frequency as a teen she and her sisters would be admonished, "Just watch yourself, I may just have to kill you!"

Ann's family was Catholic, which was an early influence in her early life. Even as a young child, perhaps no older than seven years old, Ann perceived *there must be something beyond the dogma of the Catholic Church*. To hear her recount those thoughts, "It always seemed there was way too much "blind acceptance" in the Catechism and the church rituals—and not enough taught or experienced about the love and bliss of the Divine Spirit, God." Of course, these things were perceived through her Angelic origins and memories, even though she inhabited a human body, but her parents seemed unconcerned about it.

Ann realized it was not that her parents were enthralled with Catholicism but more that they were born into it and "blindly" accepted what they had been taught by the CHURCH and THEIR parents. In the 1920's and 1930's, when Edwin and Celestial were born, this was simply how things were. People rarely questioned or strayed from their religious origins. Today, of course, things are different but there remains a prevailing belief that if you are born Catholic, you will die Catholic—even if there is no active participation in weekly Catholic Mass.

So, while Ann' family was not poor, neither was it really prosperous, by any means...but then again, this posed no problems for an Angel. Ann's mother, Celestial, was a "stay at home mom," who took care of her children. Her father, Edwin, was a beer truck driver, by which he made a good living. Unfortunately, he injured his back and forced to take a position as a shoe salesman, which left him unable to maintain the previous monetary foundation for his family. Edwin was not even a high school graduate, but was hardworking, and held a lot of love in his heart, which he openly shared with his wife and children.

During the very late forties, when Ann incarnated on Earth, it was highly unusual for a father to display these acts of love and kindness toward his children; most men simply did not want to appear soft and caring. Such traits were considered a woman's touch! Ann enjoyed these qualities of her father and she often spoke of what she found interesting, "he was an orphan and orphans very often have trouble with being intimate and loving, since usually they were not the recipients of expressed love, themselves." She also found it fascinating that, "my mother seemed "distant" at times and not highly caring about me." The fact that she got the love and caring from her father was a blessing...although one would assume it natural given that Angels are inherently blessed.

Ann sensed that, *my mother, Celestial, really did not get the loving and nurturing from her mother and thus she had never really experienced caring and loving herself.* The mystery of how her father was able to develop these traits, coming from a rather barren childhood, really impressed Ann. "It was important to me...to embark on a path of sharing, caring and loving my mother." Of course, being the qualities of an Angel...they were always naturally expressed.

For sure, Ann could easily appreciate her recent origins from the highest levels of Heaven because she found things much more loving, blissful and tranquil there! This sharp distinction paused her to question, "why are people on Earth so afraid to die and pass on since it is so much easier to live in the dimensions of Heaven?" The question was quickly followed by a realization, "it is likely the fear of going to hell and living a life of eternal damnation!" She remembered the scoffing about—and the parody of—going to hell by the inhabitants of Heaven, since everyone who had arrived knew there was no Hell, other than possibly Earth, itself, as evidenced by the many volcanoes and fire and brimstone, thereon! Ann often spoke of the amazement of those in Heaven...that anyone on Earth could believe in Hell, since it had never been astro-located by any religion, explorer or any other entity! And yet people on Earth continued to believe this misperception as something beyond doubt!

CHAPTER TWO

PLOWING THROUGH THE POOH
AN ANGEL GROWING UP IN THE CONSTRAINTS
OF THE CATHOLIC CHURCH

AS WAS MENTIONED earlier, Ann really disliked the cold and wind and the heat and humidity of Chicago and it suburbs, but she also lived in several small towns in Wisconsin, which had these same weather characteristics. But what even more disconcerting for Ann was the dead feeling and lack of love she experienced in all aspects of her interactions in the Roman Catholic Church with the priests and nuns therein.

It seemed to her that the nuns and priests—who were supposed to be God's emissaries—would be much kinder and express deeper caring and more loving qualities. Ann had forgotten about the differences from her last incarnation on Earth, long ago...versus the cooperation, love and bliss filling the higher dimensions of Heaven, where she counted on a state of non-duality and interconnectedness of all things perceived by all entities therein!

When Ann reached the age of fourteen, things became even more complicated for her; her parents began to put pressure on her to become a nun. For many Catholic families, becoming a nun or priest would be the highest purpose in life their children could achieve. Never one to shirk hard tasks while on Earth or in Heaven, Ann finally agreed to the wishes of her parents. However, she did so with the agenda to make some changes in the consciousness of the Catholic clergy by sharing the unconditional love of an Angel!

Ann entered a Catholic girl's convent high school, at Sacred Heart Convent in Indiana, at the age of fifteen; she was prepared to become a nun when she graduated from high school. She found the nuns who were her teachers cold and even mean at times; their harsh discipline often seemed sadistic to Ann. Much to her bewilderment, no matter how much Angelic love and kindness she shared with the nuns they seemed unchanged...seemingly trapped in a hierarchy that talked about the love of Jesus but really had no notion of how to manifest or express this concept.

Talking to herself, Ann pondered, "I wonder what would happen if Jesus came back to Earth? Would he even be recognized by the Catholic Church? Could he even make a difference in this rigid quasi-governmental organization?" Disconcerted about the possibilities, Ann remembered a dream she had one night where she saw a man who looked like Jesus. He had come back to Earth as a Catholic priest yet was isolated and marginalized by the bishop of the diocese where he resided! Realizing the time was neither right nor ripe for change within the Roman Catholic Church, Jesus teleported himself back to the highest domain of Heaven. *Well, that was certainly a revealing dream*, Ann thought, *but the message probably would be ignored or scoffed at by most Catholic's!*

At the end of a frustrating and demeaning year in the convent high school, Ann took stock of her situation! *Hmm*, she thought, *If Jesus failed in his mission in my dream, and I have not been able to soften the heart of even one nun here with unconditional love, is it even worth continuing to spend more time in this convent? Do I really want to be a nun? Can my presence here make any difference or have an effect in uplifting a place bereft of love? It is hard to believe I have not much uplifted this convent!*

CHAPTER THREE

MAKING LIKE A BEE AND FINDING MORE FRAGRANT FLOWERS ELSEWHERE AND ACTUALLY FINDING "SWEET FRUIT!"

ANN DECIDED THE convent she attended was more like a jail than a place of spiritual awakening and the nuns were like the "hardened" prison guards in our penal institutions. So, when she returned home for summer vacation, she told her mother and father with a determined look on her face, "I will not be returning to the convent, no matter how wonderful you think it may be or how nice it would to have me become a nun. In all my lifetimes, even in the harshness of the second dimension, I never experienced so little love and compassion for mankind in general and specifically, with the 'specific' meaning me. I am actually surprised Jesus has not come back to wipe this misguided church from the face of the Earth."

"I know you might not understand this and are probably outraged by what I am telling you, and I'm sure many Catholics will call me a heretic," Ann continued with an earnest look on her face, "but Jesus may well have already come back to Earth, worked within the priesthood, and accomplished nothing in trying to bring back the presence of love within the Roman Catholic Church that he always shared in his teachings in ancient Palestine."

"Additionally, I am certain The First and Second Council of Nicaea eliminated all overt references to reincarnation in the New Testament. If you, my parents, want to continue in the Roman Catholic Church, be my guest, but for me it is *sayonara*! There is no less Godly or spiritual place on planet Earth, and I would like to tell you why, but again, you simply could not understand! Know that as I share my experiences and perceptions with you, I have no animosity toward the Roman Catholic Church—but rather great anguish as I see how it has strayed from its purpose: to disseminate Jesus' teaching of love and compassion!"

As would be most expected, her parents, Edwin and Celestial, were quite surprised by all of Ann's statements and decisions. Actually, you could say they were befuddled by her outspoken manner, yet they knew nothing they could say would change Ann's mind. So, in an uncustomary position taken by parents in the early sixties, although they really did not agree with it, they acceded to Ann's decision. Ann's mother, Celestial, asked her, "Without the Roman Catholic Church what will you do to get religious guidance?"

An Angel Not Perceived
Dr. Robert J. Newton

Ann's reply was swift and to the point, as she stated with a tone of disgust, "I could care less if I ever have religious guidance again, although I have been reading a book, which I checked out of the library here, and it emphasizes spiritual principles over religious ones."

"Mom, I know if you experienced what I did in the convent, you would appreciate the difference between the two because the religious organizations we have lost their compasses—their direction—to the essence of spirituality and love. I remember Jesus saying, 'By their works ye shall know them!' I have tasted the 'fruit' of the Roman Catholic Church and it is very sour to the taste, and there are few if any works they have, which are of value to me, or for that matter, humanity!"

There was little Edwin and Celestial could say since at some level they knew Ann was right in her assessment, even though they would not contemplate leaving the Catholic Church, themselves, as was Ann. All the convent experience did was prod Ann to find the source or sources on Earth that would validate Jesus' teachings—and any other spiritual teachers she could find.

Ann checked out another book on comparative religions from the public library. She read about Buddhism and Hinduism and found engaging concepts therein, but these were very different from her current Christian roots. She also read from the Gnostic books about Jesus' teachings. When Ann read about Christian Science in this book, its concepts really intrigued her; she could see the essence of

17

Jesus' teachings that had been lost in the Roman Catholic Church.

Her interest was piqued! Ann shared, "then I went to a Christian Science Reading Room and after a bit of browsing, I bought the Christian Science textbook, *Science and Health with Key to the Scripture,* by Mary Baker Eddy. Therein was contained what I had been long seeking—the high spiritual principles of Love and perfection as per *Aleph Kaf Aleph*, the seventh "Name of God" from Exodus in *The Torah*, and Jesus' teachings in the Gnostic Scriptures, as found in the *Nag Hamadi* documents I had known from the high realms of Heaven." One must wonder at the myriad epiphanies and insights which came to Ann's consciousness as she recalled the memories of her former abode in the high Heavens.

Most of the things Ann read in *Science and Health…*were verified, based on her prior heavenly knowledge. Especially germane to Ann was the fact that everything was spirit and that all matter was simply an illusion. That meant everything was basically energy as opposed to dense matter! Someone from the high realms of Heaven could really appreciate that, because it described exactly how things work in Heaven and on Earth as well—although most humans scoff at the concept as being contrary to reality, and quite delusional, too wit. Ann had smiled when Mrs. Eddy, the founder of Christian Science and the author of *Science and Health,* declared, "It is possible to live in a state of Heaven on Earth". That is what Ann's mission to Earth was about, she realized. She knew firsthand the very insights of Mrs. Eddy and anything similar thereto. She knew *she had found a bit of "sweet fruit" on Earth of which she would partake!*

As Ann entered her first year of high school, she caught the eye of a cocky young teenager, Gregor, who just happened to have a '54 Buick Sedan with a Dynaflow™ transmission. Ann was quite stunningly beautiful, but shy and reserved, so when Gregor introduced himself to her, she was attracted to his rugged Polish good looks, and being new to the school, was reassured to have a pal to show her around. In a short time, they were dating as boyfriend and girlfriend—and due to Gregor's persistence in the matter— it was not long before the couple became sexually intimate,

Obviously, most teenage males are so horny that most of their life centers on finding sex and/or having a sexual consort. Ann found the sexual encounter interesting and not nasty or forbidden but realized Gregor had no knowledge of the higher energy aspects of sexuality other than his own ejaculation and the ensuing orgasm. Even in the highest realms of Heaven there are energy exchanges similar to sexual intercourse on Earth, but it centers on the exchange of Pranic energy (God Force) through the hands and Chakra energy centers rather than sexual organs.

Ann's sexual exploration with Gregor ended, although she continued to date him. Understandably, Gregor was less than thrilled about her decision, but Ann convinced him she did not want to get pregnant and since he was not using condoms, pregnancy for her was not an option...but it was a real possibility, if they continued to have unprotected sex.

She did appreciate the fact that Gregor's Buick had one of the first automatic transmissions, of any car model ever built and he even let her drive his car a little bit. But that was not enough for Ann to continue with Gregor sexually, since he did not believe in "safe sex" or bothering to use a condom!

CHAPTER FOUR

LEARNING MORE THAN BEFORE AS THE "GYPSY" MOTHER MOVES THE FAMILY TO CALIFORNIA

AT THE END of the high school year, Ann bid Gregor, adieu, as her mother had an "itch"—actually a strong urge—to move the family to California. Celestial convinced Edwin California offered far more opportunities and potential fortunes than where they currently resided in Chicago. Moving was a recurring theme with Celestial; she always saw the grass on the other side of the hill as greener. She also convinced Edwin they would be better off living in a more temperate climate. Ann was certainly amenable to California move, but was reminded how impossible it had been for her to develop any long-term friends or boyfriends, because the family had moved so many times in the past!

In this ensuing move, Ann asked her mother, "Why are we always moving?"

Celestial responded in a state of optimism, with a wry smile "I am always hoping we can have a more prosperous life and own a home, rather than always renting!"

Ann replied, unable to withhold her sarcastic overtones "How has that worked out so far, huh, Mom? Obviously, not so well! With all the many places we have lived, it seems to me we are actually worse off rather than better."

"You might be right!" Ann's mother exclaimed, "But I still believe our family will find good fortune in California and you will too!"

To an extent, that would eventually be true, but certainly not at first. Of course, for an Angel, anything is possible! Yet the limitations of a human body made everything more difficult and complicated as once again Ann and her siblings were thrown into new schools, without any previous friends. Ann attended a very wealthy high school—Villa Park High, even though she lived in a middle-class area in Orange, California.

Unfortunately for Ann, the students at Villa Park had no knowledge of her Angelic origins and seemed to find delight as they spurned her because her clothes were not of a designer origin or anything close thereto! Heaven forbid any student at this school wear anything other than designer clothes. Years later, there would be conversations by others who were present, about the "norm" of having been snubbed, and treated as "less than." Ann's lot was to have but one close girlfriend and eventually a boyfriend, named Larry.

During her senior year at Villa Park High, Ann went to the Senior Prom with Larry; she found him to be very much in his head—interested in technical things—and thus more aloof rather than caring and loving! For most women this kind of relationship would be a problematic situation, but Ann understood that an Angel loves unconditionally, so there was no need to take issue...she also didn't have any other romantic prospects at that point in time.

During this "upheaval" period of her life, Ann continued studying the Christian Science textbook, *Science and Health with Key to the Scripture*, by Mary Baker Eddy. Watching Ann's avid interest, eventually her mother began to study the book as well. It was no surprise to discover Christian Science was the diametric opposite of The Roman Catholic Church. It was an awakening for Ann's mother to read as Mary Baker Eddy described a state of Heaven therein that could be manifested on Earth; the same beliefs Ann kept resonating with. She came to understand how someone who had just descended from heaven could and would appreciate the wisdom—immeasurably more than her contemporaries, and then some! *Why would the Roman Catholic Church hide this*? Ann questioned. She was so befuddled by this omission, and further pondered, *since it has access to a Vatican Library, with books containing this liberating information, the irony of this is too stark to ignore...at least for me, but apparently not them!*

Shortly after Ann's high school graduation, her family bought a modest house in Costa Mesa, California and Ann and her mother began attending The First Church of Christ Scientist, Costa Mesa, California. *What a complete difference in the atmosphere in a Christian Science Church*, Ann thought. *Here, I feel the Spirit of God and Jesus, and a loving, supportive atmosphere. I never felt that in a Catholic Mass. It was little more than going through the motions, which actually is quite the opposite! I guess there are a lot of people who attend mass who do not feel the difference; I can only think it is because the attendees at Mass just go through the motions in a rote manner. They have grown comfortable with an unemotional state of obligation rather than devotion, although every once and a while, I see a few people at Mass that seem to be engrossed in Jesus and God!*

Life always has its way of moving on; Ann secured a job as a bookkeeper in a menswear store, owned by a Jewish businessman, Dewey, where she not only learned things about business, but also about Jewish culture and religion. Additionally, she met a young man, Conner, who attended the same church she attended, who was very drawn to Ann's beauty and soft-spoken personality. Connor was very cocky and sure of himself on the outside yet seemed to have the perpetual need to be stoned on Cannabis. Ann was not aware of this until she went a date with Connor to a Doors concert, where he smoked Cannabis all night long.

An Angel Not Perceived
Dr. Robert J. Newton

For Angels, such a need for a tranquilizer like Marijuana is unnecessary, because they live in the strong presence of the Lord and do not need such medication. Ann tried to share with Connor how Cannabis was not really necessary to live a tranquil and fulfilling life, but he was not interested in something he considered babble. Ann asked him, "Do you think this is a part of Christian Science? Certainly, your parents are drug and alcohol-free, as you only know too well!"

Connor just laughed as he threw his head backward, "My parents really do not get it. They live a boring life and I lead an exciting one so I will continue to do what I do!"

Ann then replied, "Well with that as your perspective, I am out of here. I wish you the best and hope you change your perspective about your Cannabis medication!"

This incident would tinge the rest of Ann's life as an incarnated Angel; she held fast to her belief that Cannabis inhibited a person's ability to have a direct and strong connection to their Creator, so they could ascend to the highest levels of Heaven. It was not that Cannabis was inherently bad, but that it created an artificial connection to God that could never be sustained in Heaven! Ann knew to remain in the highest realms of Heaven a person must have strong connection to the light of the Creator, as per the 59th Name of God, *Hey Resh Chet*.

Again, beliefs such as Ann held would be dismissed and marginalized by many people throughout the later sixties when Marijuana, although illegal, was smoked by most of the young people of the time. It was the "in thing" to do! It was the drug *du jour*...much more so than alcohol!

Luckily for Ann, she would soon meet a soul mate with whom she could strongly resonate with...without the influence of Cannabis!

CHAPTER FIVE

TRANSCENDING THE JIVE AND CREATING A HIGH VIBE, THE WAY ONLY AN ANGEL CAN!

ANN WOULD SOON meet her soul mate/twin flame sooner than she realized but interestingly enough, they almost did not upon first appearances, get together romantically! Ann had met James after a Sunday service at the Costa Mesa Christian Science Church, where he came to participate in a Christian Science Youth Group. The group was having a dance party and James was extremely interested in meeting Ann there and expressed his desire to her.

They agreed to meet there on Friday night. Ann could have gauged James' interest in the fact that he showed up at 7:30 P.M. Unfortunately, Ann forgot to tell James she would not be at the party until 9:30 P.M. because she was working at the menswear store, where she was employed. Dismayed that Ann skipped the party, he started dancing with another young woman who was petite and very cute! James really did not intend to become involved with this woman, Phyllis, however, the more songs they danced together the closer they became enmeshed...entranced enthralled with each other, likewise.

Imagine the surprise when Ann showed up at 9:30, only to see James with Phyllis and James—likewise—surprised to see her. A conversation between the two ensued, where James was able to explain to Ann his disappointment at thinking she would not show up. He heard Ann's explanation about work, and saw by her expression she was disappointed about him linking up with Phyllis but by that time he felt locked into Phyllis's energy that evening and wasn't confident things would materialize with Ann. He did, however, bolster his options by getting Ann's phone number from his friend, Randel; he was aware that as much as he enjoyed Phyllis, he liked Ann even more!

Despite his great night with Phyllis, the next day, James called Ann. He again explained what happened and told her he wanted to take her out on a date Saturday evening. Ann replied, "I thought you were no longer interested in me since you were so intimate with Phyllis—dancing and hugging and kissing her."

Feeling suddenly discomforted by the thought of having lost a chance with Ann, James told her, "I was disappointed when I got to the party and you were not there and after waiting awhile, Phyllis came up to me and asked me to dance with her. I said, yes because I thought you were not coming to the party. I beg you, Ann, cut me some slack on this. I promise to make you laugh this evening...that IS my specialty, that AND being very handsome!" James laughed hysterically as he talked about how handsome he was, and was pleased to see that Ann was likewise.

"I guess I will give you another chance, Goofy James," Ann replied. "But I sure thought you were going to be dating Phyllis, the way you both were clinging to each other!"

"Thank you, Ann," James exclaimed, heaving a big sigh of relief. "You will not regret it and I hope you like pizza! I would much rather be with you than Phyllis! You were my first choice all along!"

"I do," Ann responded, "as long as it is Ooh pizza!"

"Then Mr. Ooh's Pizza it is," James replied.

James picked up Ann at her house in Costa Mesa that evening, and they drove in his car to Mr. Ooh's Pizza in Newport Beach, enjoying the Pacific Coast Highway, whose natural beauty held them both breathless in its beauty.

All during the simple pizza dinner, James couldn't shift his focus from just how beautiful the blonde-haired Ann was. And beyond her obvious beauty, James experienced an Angelic presence that completely captivated him. Even though he didn't know at that time Ann had, in fact, descended from the Angelic realms of Heaven to the domain of Earth. But then, he would figure that out sooner than later!

An Angel Not Perceived
Dr. Robert J. Newton

He paid more attention to their conversation than eating his pizza and when James took a bite from his piece some extra cheese pulled from where he bit into the crust and the very hot cheese got stuck on his chin. The pain was intense! James yelped in pain, "Ooh, ooh, ooh, ooh!"

When James finally wiped the hot pizza from his chin Ann asked, "What just happened to you…. are you a spazz or something—or are you trying to tell me you love Mr. Ooh's Pizza?"

"Both," James said laughing, "but really now, have a bit of compassion! I just burned my chin with that hot pizza cheese."

"Well in that case," Ann declared, "you are not a spazz! I was worried there for a minute!"

"Worry no more," James responded, "I am only goofy!"

"That is immeasurably better" Ann stated, laughing out loud!

For sure, two people have rarely ever gotten along better on a first date. Although Ann did not smile a lot because she had extra teeth in her mouth, James could not care less, and he knew that night, without a doubt, he was going to do everything in his power to marry her. Ann really liked James too; she enjoyed his humor, his goofiness, and his smile…even though she perceived James was very immature which later proved a correct evaluation! There was not only the fact that neither of them smoked marijuana, nor drank alcoholic beverages, but certainly a lot of other common factors to bring them together. Most importantly, each was enthralled with Christian Science, since they were both aware it had helped them get through some very critical situations in their lives.

In James case, he knew at the age of five the Christian doctrine of flawed sinners who needed redemption made no sense at all. In Sunday School at Bethel Baptist Church, James was told "God is Love" and then in the church service Reverend Roman was telling him he was going to hell if he did not accept Jesus Christ as his savior and repent for his sins. The disparity between these two concepts was too blatant for James to dismiss. *How could God love me and then condemn me*, James thought. *Love and condemnation to a fiery fate are* **not consistent—they are diametric opposites!**

No one James knew seemed to perceive this concern; he felt continually more isolated...the deepening consideration to commit suicide washed over him, like a wave plunging against the California shoreline. Being introduced to the Christian Science textbook, *Science and Health with Key to the Scripture*, allowed James to see there were other people who perceived what he did. This awareness was a great relief since he realized he was not CRAZY as he had previously been told many times—so many times he started to believe it himself!

Eventually James would gain some clear insights about Ann's Angelic origins and be open to sharing his belief she WAS an Angel. He was not saying this to gain some romantic advantage but because it was a heartfelt sentiment. Ann just slightly smiled and thanked James saying, "Finally my identity has been perceived by one person on Earth. It certainly took long enough for that to happen! Anyway, I just find you so much fun to be with…you were not exaggerating as to your humor and wit. Additionally, you are a smarty pants for sure!"

Interestingly enough, Ann had already figured James was of extraterrestrial origin and in fact, that he was from the Planet Sirius "B". This was a fifth-dimension planet, so it already existed in the realms of Heaven, but not as high as the Angelic realms of Heaven. So, for James to incarnate into Earth was akin to Ann's incarnation into Earth from Angelic Heaven! In both cases, Ann and James had chosen to come to Earth, on a humanitarian mission, to set the stage for the manifestation of Heaven on Earth, as perceived by Mary Baker Eddy in *Science and Health*, and as was mentioned before—other things related to this manifestation!

They were a good match, two oddballs—odd Ducks— operating outside of the normal parameters of living on planet Earth. True, James was very energetic, and sports oriented, while Ann was tranquil and into things involving the arts. But from these differences each was able to share and teach the other! You might wonder what more they might have to learn from each other, considering the lofty dimensions from which they came to Earth but both of them knew learning is a continual, eternal process. As James often proclaimed, "God is always learning and so should humans, likewise! Otherwise, they will get left in the dust!"

An Angel Not Perceived

Dr. Robert J. Newton

As the romance bloomed, Ann and James spent as much time together as possible. He would take Ann to the beach, go surfing and try to "show off" or start a fire in a fire ring, make dinner for her, and then enjoy fire and marshmallows after dinner. Late at night, they would stroll and dance on the beach. The feeling they experienced when in each other's arms and dancing was sublime and exciting for both of them. The embraces, hugging and kissing activated their hearts, which created and released a field of energy that bonded deeper each time they met! Ann was completely focused on James—James was enamored with Ann!

After three months of intensive dating, James wrapped up one of their dates on the steps of Ann's parent's house by asking Ann to marry him. Although James was very scared to take this step, he was madly in love with Ann and quite sure she would say yes. Imagine how devastated James was when Ann responded, "I'm just not yet ready to marry!" James broke into tears, which prompted Ann to tell him, "I still want to date you and I hope we will continue doing that." She was quite enthralled with James but thought he was not mature enough for marriage. James responded to Ann and said, "I still want to marry you. I want to be with you!"

The couple continued dating and not too soon after she had turned him down, Ann was house-sitting for the mother of Dewey, her boss. She asked James to come over so they could spend the night together. When James arrived at the house in Lakewood, he knocked on the door; when Ann opened it, she threw her arms around James and surprised him with a very passionate and lengthy kiss. The excitement drove them to the couch, where the kissing continued and fondling ensued. Ann gave way to the passion that fueled romantic actions. She didn't mind the least leaving James with the promise of a well-worn cliché, "Wait here on the couch while I go and get into something more comfortable." James didn't mind in the least when a minute or so later Ann returned in a silk negligee.

Ann was compelled to share her truth with James, buffering the fact that she was not a virgin, but wanted him to know she wanted to be intimate with him and fully consummate their relationship. She reminded him, "I was "with Gregor, the boyfriend I've talked about before. He was not interested in safe sex and I was naïve, but not enough to want to get pregnant by him!"

"Well," James replied, "the past is the past and anyway I had oral sex with a girlfriend I told you about. So, things are more or less equal since neither of us is really a virgin."

"That makes me feel very happy," Ann responded, "since I care about you very much…much more than you might believe."

"Meeting you and the way you understand and care about me has been a Godsend." James replied. "An Angel deserves no less and I am so blessed to have you in my life and experience your Angelic presence…every day with you is a joy supreme"

An Angel Not Perceived
Dr. Robert J. Newton

Although Ann had very little sexual experience in her current incarnation, she certainly knew how to surrender to James in a state of relaxation...relying on the intense love growing within her heart. James, who had never experienced full penetration with a woman, brought great passion from his heart also, and surrendered to Ann, likewise. Together, they discovered that when two hearts come together as theirs did, a rare and special magic occurred wherein both partners allow a state of bliss and euphoria that transcended their orgasms. Yes, they both had intense orgasms, yet they paled in significance to the high dimensions the lovers ascended to as a result of their combined sexual energy...an intense Kundalini experience, which lasted for hours!

In the afterglow of sexual chemistry, which produces great amounts of electricity when a sensual event of a great magnitude occurs, a "doorway" is opened to the higher levels of the fifth-dimension and beyond—wherein the middle levels of heaven occur. And that is just where Ann and James were transported, even though their bodies were in the third-dimension, on Earth.

This fifth-dimension was something both Ann and James had experienced before they decided to incarnate on Earth: Ann in the very highest level of Heaven, in the Ninth Paradise on the ninth-dimension of heaven and James on the planet, Sirius "B," in the fifth-dimension.

Nevertheless, the most important point relative to the couple's experience, irrespective of the scientific aspects, is that in the afterglow of their sexual union, Ann and James were locked into an embrace where the energy of true love was incubated and expanded. What they felt most people would call true love, but those words are incapable of conveying the levels of divinity James and Ann experienced. Truly, what the couple experienced was something beyond a cogent explanation and being an experiential thing...much beyond words!

CHAPTER SIX

CREATING A GREAT UNION FROM THE ASHES OF A PREVIOUS ENCOUNTER

SOON AFTER the magical night, the passionate encounter, Ann suggested to James they get married. Of course, James was overcome with joy; this is what he wanted from the first time he set eyes on the Angelic Ann. Likewise, Ann, of course, had come to embrace the very intense feelings she had for James.

"I just have one condition to our marriage, James," Ann shared in a voice with trepidation, "I do not want to have children, because I do not think I am capable of bringing a fetus to term."

"Well," James sympathetically responded, "I really do not want to have children either. Considering all the heartache both of us experienced growing up, for me, it does not make sense to bring more people into this world, so your condition is not a deal breaker, Ann!"

"Wow," Ann declared, "you took a huge burden off my shoulders... I was sure you would reject my condition for our marriage!"

One thing had been revealed to both Ann and James: they knew each other in at least one previous incarnation on Earth. How they came to these conclusions, independent of each other, was through dreams each had at night, as well as small and large blurbs of information and pictures, which surfaced from intuitional hunches and insights—in their minds. In fact, Ann and James would learn over time that they previously been together as a couple—many times— and were, indeed, soulmates...twin flames who cultivated feelings for each other through these many incarnations.

Before they were married James shared his sentiments about the impending event, saying, "You know, Ann, I would be actually happier if we skipped the public marriage ceremony and just eloped."

To this, Ann replied, "I would agree with you except my family would prefer we have a public ceremony."

"Well, I am sure my parents feel the same way, but I would prefer to elope but, in the end, I want you to be comfortable and happy about the marriage so we will do it your way.

An Angel Not Perceived

Dr. Robert J. Newton

James had to fulfill his National Guard active duty commitment before he would marry Ann, so the wedding occurred a few months after fulfilling his basic and infantry training in the Army—at a beautiful mortuary chapel, with less than a hundred guests.

People kept asking James if he was nervous or having second thoughts about the upcoming marriage ceremony and he repeatedly responded, "Are you crazy? I look forward to being united in marriage with Ann. She is special beyond all imaginable words! I am nervous about nothing and in fact in a state of euphoria. I realize just how fortunate I am to have her in my life."

So obviously James was relaxed and smiling during the wedding ceremony. Ann, too, was calm and collected and looking forward to her life with him. She had picked a beautiful mortuary chapel which allowed couples to have weddings in the evening. Better yet there was no fee, which was very fortuitous since neither Ann nor James had any savings; James could barely pay for the upcoming honeymoon in Carmel, California. The couple also felt fortunate that Ann's mother, Celestial, held a very modest wedding reception at her house, which saved them even more money.

Their simple wedding was in stark contrast to the high-priced galas today, which are more about production and spectacle rather than a focus on the love between a couple. For Ann and James, all the fluff was inconsequential since they were solely focused on their love for each other.

The love they felt surfaced as the ceremony culminated in James giving Ann an extremely long kiss and more kisses after that! The short and stylish wedding gown Ann had chosen kept James excited, making it hard for him to control himself and move onto the wedding reception. The attention James paid to Ann was so obvious her sisters implored, "You guys need to get a room!"

To which James replied in his off-handed manner, "We do not need a room since we have an apartment."

The reception was at Ann's parents' house and again was a simple and low-key event, with Ann's mother making the food for the occasion. James looked across the room and glancing at Ann in her gown, thought, *this food is nothing for us to get excited about but for sure—although I don't particularly care for my mother-in-law—I just can't get out of my mind the appreciation for all her sewing talent that went into Ann's simple, stylish, beautiful wedding gown.*

After the wedding reception, James and Ann went to their new apartment and spent the first night there. At the apartment, Ann queried James, "Do you mind if we do not have sex tonight? We just had it last night and I am very tired from the events of the evening."

Ann knew she could count on the response from James, "Well I was looking forward to what the night would bring... you know I find it very hard to resist you! Yet I understand your physical limitations and what more to enjoy if we are both rested up and consummate our "union" tomorrow night in Carmel.

The next morning found the couple with every sense in high pitch as they drove up the coastline; they were both in a state of bliss, talking about how grateful each was to have met the other and finally, the completed hearts, joined in love as a married couple.

The honeymoon was more than James could have envisioned. In Carmel, he came to realize Ann was even more special than he had previously perceived. *I don't know how to put this into words; I can feel it! I've never been with Ann for more than a weekend. This week-long honeymoon is expanding my perception and appreciation of this magical woman!*

Since James couldn't articulate what he felt, virtually no one else was aware of the depth of his feelings for Ann...including Ann's parents—nor James' mother and father. James pondered this for a time, as he watched Ann sleeping, and recognized it was his psychic ability... the clairsentience James had come to understand the nuances of Ann; he was unaware of this psychic ability early in his life!

Spending an entire week at the beach for their honeymoon was a really wonderful experience, even though James agreed he would not do any surfing on their honeymoon, as per Ann's request! She looked across the room at her new husband and thought, *I am so fortunate to have someone who will support me—emotionally and spiritually—a need that has rarely been met by my family at home.*

Unfortunately, shortly after the honeymoon when the couple had returned to their apartment in Costa Mesa, James began arguing with Ann about how things should be in their lives and who should be the decision-maker about the things in their life. James, of course, thought he should have the "last word" on things because he was the man in the relationship, and Ann held an equally strong position that their decisions should be mutually decided.

It took James several months to finally relent to Ann on this decision-making matter. Apparently, he did not realize that you can never really win against an Angel, no matter how convincing your arguments were. James' mind slowly morphed as he learned to let go of his last vestiges of paternalistic, chauvinistic behavior. What James did not realize was that this would be one of many lessons he would learn from Ann—and his life would be very enriched by living in her presence!

CHAPTER SEVEN

GETTING THINGS FIXED WITH THIS NEW MIX
AND TRYING TO CREATE HEAVEN ON EARTH

JUST LIKE IN baking a cake, mixing the right ingredients give a sweeter result, so the same thing happens when two people learn to mix their lives harmoniously. That can only happen when there is a mutual approach to things as was Ann's way...

Once James acceded to a harmonious approach to life, things became sweeter in the coupled life of Ann and James. It became quickly evident that letting an Angel "win" actually benefitted James, since selfishness is not a quality of an Angel. In the larger scope of their lives James actually "won" by losing his ego, whilst Ann really had no ego to lose!

Both Ann and James worked very hard in low paying jobs—James as a clerk in a supermarket stocking shelves and Ann as a bookkeeper and office manager in a men's clothing store. James' position provided medical benefits through the Retail Clerk's Union and a bit of overtime work. Ann, on the other hand, had few benefits and worked six days a week. Her boss and owner of the men's store apparently was ignorant of her ANGEL origins and expected a lot of work for low wages. James often wondered whether her boss would have treated her differently if he knew of her exalted origins and presence? But conceding he probably would not, since he seemed to be trapped in the stereotypical attitudes of many Jewish merchants in the early 1970's—who thought women were not entitled to equal wages as those paid to men. Eventually, through hard work, the couple would come to have earnings that provided an easier and more comfortable life, as a result of joining their efforts to "getting ahead" in life.

James ultimately decided to enroll in law school, since he knew he needed to make more money than was possible working in a grocery store. This meant going to school three evenings a week and working the grocery store's graveyard shift. Aside from the personal strain of limited time this created in James' life, including his once a month weekend obligation in the California Army National Guard, it meant Ann and James would have little time to spend together. They had to be creative and ingenious to carve out time to be together, not only romantically but leisurely as well!

James asked Ann, "Are you sure it is alright that I go to law school since it will surely 'squeeze' us time wise? I do not mind the work burden myself, but I do not want our relationship to wither and die!"

"Well, James, we both agree that you will be a great attorney since you like to argue—hint, hint—so I am good with our decision!"

"I am more interested in creating justice and equality for all people on Earth rather than arguing," James replied. "But I do not want all of that to get "between" us.

The couple was determined to work hard on their relationship…James grabbing what moments he could stopping by in the evenings at Ann's job at Chasins Men's Store. And in other little snippets of time, they would catch meals at various restaurants in the South Coast Plaza Mall. These moments, and the occasional weekend dance clubs made it work!

James faced a real personal growth in understanding his love for another human being! He loved to surf any chance he got, but he discovered the depths of his love for the Angelic Ann and knew he could never get enough of her. In light of the demands on his time, he embraced the reality that if it took being flexible and creative to have more of her time, so be it! He felt no qualms about a summer vacation limited to one weekend someplace in California, as opposed to some distant and exotic location!

As for romance, this too was mostly limited to weekends and so rather than Ann or James complaining about this, they simply took the opportunities they had and made the best of it. Theirs was not one of those relationships where the man always put his interests and pleasures before those of his woman. Despite his early chauvinistic tendencies, James always knew that in romance, the woman should always be pleased either BEFORE the man—or simultaneously WITH the man.

James was pondering this one late evening as he headed out to meet Ann, and found he was talking to himself! "How I knew about this need to satisfy Ann first, I don't know! At first, it was kind of an intuitive thing."

Later, James would learn his knowledge stemmed from past life experiences. Irrespective of the beginning of James' awareness, Ann appreciated beyond all words having a sensitive and caring man who made romance and sexuality a wonderful and blissful experience as opposed to something where her partner was just going through the motions.

Ann once asked James, "How and where did you learn the advanced things about romance and sexuality you know? You always make me feel so special and I know from personal experience and the experiences other women talk about that what you do is so rare!"

"I can assure you, Ann, this is in fact a rare thing most men either do not perceive or care about," James replied. "As I have told you before, what I do is intuitive and comes from my heart. Having you as my wife, just how special and beautiful you are, makes me want to bring great pleasure into your life wherever and whenever I can. I can assure you that despite whatever I give to you, it gets returned to me in a multiplied fashion."

"I don't know about that, "Ann exclaimed. "Things seem to be even matched from my perspective."

"And so, I would expect my ANGEL to say nothing less," James replied, "since you are humble, and this is something few people on this planet can muster and/or understand!"

"You must understand, whatever I do with you, Ann, I really enjoy it. The fact you often do not feel good, health wise and/or pain wise, you still do not let it affect you very much at all. Even if it as simple as when I am with you when we attend the Christian Science Church in Corona del Mar, I enjoy it immensely."

"The fact we are learning things and expanding our spiritual knowledge, means a lot to me too!" Ann replied. Mary Baker Eddy shared so many things with us in *Science and Health with Key to the Scripture*, I wonder if we will ever completely understand what she knew."

"I have this feeling," James responded, "that you already know these things from your previous incarnations, especially those you spent in heaven with your ANGELIC companions."

"I would never sell you short on this either, James. I have really had a lot of really good insights from things you have shared with me!"

"We are just *muy simpatico*!" James blurted out loud.

CHAPTER EIGHT

MAKING THINGS GREAT
WITH HEAVEN IN SIGHT!

LIFE WAS GOOD; this union was solid, sound, and filled with mutual love. In the second year of their marriage, James quit his job in the grocery store to build his own landscaping, gardening and tree trimming business. This allowed him to work for himself, which greatly suited his independent nature.

Ann on the other hand, was locked into what most people would consider a "dead end" job. Rather than complain about this or the fact her boss was very demanding yet not compensating her commensurately for her hard work and dedication to his business, Ann graciously moved forward! Again, that is just the nature of ANGELS!

Why Ann would operate so graciously under these circumstances was hard for James to even understand because of the inherent inequities that resulted from her circumstances. From James' and even Ann's perspective, there are always people who want to take advantage of a situation and not pay people in respect to their abilities and production! In one of their conversations, James noted to Ann, "It is like replacing a borrowed full loaf of bread with a half a loaf." But they both understood that things just don't add up and the people paying substandard remuneration really know what they are doing is not fair...they choose to label it as fair and part of doing business. Don't take it personally, they say... it's just business!

Ann was quite excited about helping James build a landscaping business; she did his bookkeeping, gave him many good business insights, and even created the name for his business, "Joyous James' Landscaping." Ann selected the name with some thought on the 39th Name of God from "Exodus," *Resh Hey Ayin,* that she would share with James many years later. It simply means, "finding the good in the bad."

By maintaining an attitude of always finding the good in the bad, Ann and James scaled many obstacles in their future, both emotional and physical. James thought about Ann one day...about the unique things that set her apart from most other humans on Earth, and recognized, *That's it! She is never distracted by the small picture or the minute details therein. She focuses on life's big pictures and what can be accomplished from a more positive perspective.* In that one small moment, he understood the lofty perch in Heaven previously occupied by Ann, contributed to her holistic perspective. *Maybe,* James thought, *the lesson in this is to always for us to focus our perspective in the heavens which Ann always mentions is attainable through a regular practice of prayer and meditation, and in fact what she does!*

Time was drawing close for James to graduate from law school when he realized he would rather continue to pursue his landscaping business. He couldn't seem to discuss the matter with Ann because he didn't want to experience her being disappointed with him. And disappointed she was when James finally "spilled the beans" but she supported his decision and never complained that he probably could make more money as an attorney. Her gracious behavior again was consistent with the way ANGELS operate. James wrapped himself in this blessing as he thought, *Angels just do not complain! Rather, they always find the good in the bad.* And then, he quietly said to himself, "This might be because really there is no bad…that the Creator was incapable of making anything bad even though many religious texts and teachers tell us otherwise!"

Life for this dynamic duo continued to be blessed. After several years, James' landscape company was well positioned and profitable, which afforded the ability to buy nice cars and jewelry and go on vacations with Ann. They had wisely bought a house in the second year of their marriage by scraping enough money together to get an FHA-VA Loan and borrowing money from Ann's boss.

An Angel Not Perceived

Dr. Robert J. Newton

Ann looked at life beyond the enjoyment of James' gifts; the spiritual progress and the expanded spiritual knowledge she was attaining were much more important. Much of this knowledge came to Ann outside of their Christian Science Church knowledge. At some point, James protested Ann going outside her Christian Science foundation to pursue other occult and esoteric sources. He was not ready to make a change or leave Christian Science even though he was "hitting a wall" therein, as had Ann. He was forced to admit, *I'm no longer finding the inspiration in "Science and Health," the Christian Science textbook, like I was previously, when I first discovered it!*

What James did not realize was that all Ann was learning would help him in the not too distant future… more than he could fathom. He had just never considered the remote possibility that Ann was investigating these other spiritual disciplines because she too had "hit a spiritual wall."

And in fact, this "reveal" would happen in a way James could not foresee! He was involved in a bad dirt motorcycle accident when just thirty-five. Although James refused to go to the hospital to be examined and treated as Ann counseled him to do, she still supported his decision and helped James manifest a spiritual healing, as per the Christian Science protocols. Although James experienced physical healing, the accident created a lot of emotional turbulence in his life. James could not understand why he was involved in such a severe accident and in asking Ann about his feelings, he burst forth emotionally, "I do not really understand why this freakish accident happened to me! Do you have any insights into this, Ann?"

"I do have some insights, James, but I think the best idea would be for you to confer with a psychic about your questions. There is a psychic fair at the Psynetics Foundation this weekend and we should probably go there if you are up to it!"

"You have to know, Ann, all of this feels just a bit weird for me—you know, going to psychics and similar things. But I am so 'thrown for a loop' about my accident, I will try anything that will give me understanding and insight into these questions that keep surfacing in my mind!"

Sunday morning came, and Ann and James were off to the psychic fair at the Psynetics Foundation. Luckily for him, Ann was in command of the situation because James had no idea what he was doing and to him, the whole scene seemed like something reminiscent of a "Love-in" from the sixties. He even entertained a few vivid visuals of people wearing psychedelic inspired clothing. Ann surveyed the room of psychics at the "fair" and then told James, "I think there is a person here who can "read you." See that older woman in the middle of the room with the purple scarf on her head?"

James appeared hesitant, and Ann was somewhat taken aback by his powerful response, "I don't know what the hell is going on here but let the fun and the freak show begin".

An Angel Not Perceived

Dr. Robert J. Newton

James approached the chosen psychic, whose name turned out to be Gloria Jane, and as he got close, she asked him, "Can I help you?"

Feeling the need to be totally honest, James replied, "I have never done this before and do not even know if I believe in psychics but let's see if you can tell me about what happened to me recently!"

Gloria closed her eyes for a couple of minutes, awaiting psychic impressions, and finally replied, "You have recently been hurt in a very bad motorcycle accident. Did you go to a hospital yet?"

"No! I haven't gone to a hospital and have no intention of doing so," James responded in a somewhat indignant manner.

"Well, you most certainly need to," Gloria said, "You see, young man, you have internal injuries and bleeding."

"Oh, I can assure you that was true following the accident, "James exclaimed, "but I've mostly healed myself!"

Of course, the ANGELIC Ann agreed with Gloria's psychic reading, but this was one of the few times James knew more about what was going on than Ann. One would have thought James probably would never have consulted a psychic again but within a week he went to Gloria at her house to get more insight into his accident. And again, Gloria reiterated her warning that James needed to go to a hospital—and yet again, James told her he was most definitely not in need of a doctor or hospitals.

The bigger question on James' mind was why he even had the accident. When he asked Gloria if she knew the underlying "why," she gave him the same response Ann had given numerous times, "You were being impatient!" James paused a moment and thought to himself, *Wow! again, yet another example of the highly developed psychic abilities of an* ANGEL *as well as a psychic.* But in the end, James fully embraced that both of them had correctly ascertained the issue of James' impatience.

One good outcome of James' accident was how it allowed Ann an opening to be able to take James into an expanded spiritual perspective beyond Christian Science. True, James, because of his extraterrestrial origins, had high spiritual knowledge but a lot of this was obscured because of his incarnation to Earth! Ann was less limited in this way, because of her exalted Angelic origins, and her mind was constantly probing new subjects and areas to investigate! Ann knew the Psynetics Foundation had just the classes that would bring James "up to speed" with her understanding and knowledge.

Now, this is where things got really interesting since James had thus far limited his focus to reincarnation, psychic abilities, astrology, numerology and vegetarianism. These were things in which Ann had already become proficient, making it a joyful experience to have her soul mate and companion open and willing to gravitate to and flourish in the things most people would never venture into.

One might ask why Ann even had to learn these things again, considering her high ANGELIC origins. It was simply one of those things related to "the veil," which means most—or at least a considerable amount of the information we have from other incarnations and dimensions, is hidden from us when we incarnate on Earth. Sometimes the extraordinary talents we hold are brought forward into new incarnations but almost never the past knowledge we had....at least in a clear and open manner. It is up to us to rediscover and hone and talents in the current incarnation in which we reside!

James found comfort that his spouse and lover could help him bring these things forward, and for the "impatient" James, he knew it would be in an accelerated fashion. James knew no one could have a better teacher for this than he did.

While Ann would never attain any significant fame for her knowledge and abilities, James often wondered how this beautiful and magnificent woman could be overlooked by society at large. He began think, *hmmm, someday I may have to share this Angelic being in a book I just might have to write in the future.*

Because of his new studies, James felt it was imperative he learned to meditate. Ann tried to help him with this but for sure, James had trouble sitting in one place for any longer than a few minutes. Ann suggested James read Ram Dass' book on meditation, *Journey of Awakening: A Meditator's*

Guidebook, and told him she was sure he would be able to mediate after reading this book. Indeed, this book really did help James as he realized that meditation could happen during sports, running, walking, dancing and even things like sewing and artistic endeavors. For some reason, after realizing he was meditating during activities he pursued, especially surfing, James was able to sit down and meditate. He was so grateful for the guidance of Ann and realized he might have never learned to do a sit-down mediation without her help.

In fact, Ann and James would eventually learn to meditate at a level usually only Buddhist monks experience! Meanwhile, as Ann and James were progressing into deeper spiritual knowledge, they also became exposed to Tantric and Taoist sexual practices. This approach to sexuality attuned the partners to the energy involved, as opposed to just "fun with friction". James had an intuitive knowledge of these things from previous incarnations but getting "reacquainted" with this knowledge made his romantic unions even more intense. For Ann, it meant deeper orgasms and a way to truly share the energies of her heart with James. For Ann and James, sexuality was always much beyond having children. It was about the bonding of two hearts and the more they merged sexually, the more this heart bonding was fostered.

Ann and James both agreed that they did not want children and that they could have a deeper and more meaningful relationship with each other without them! In fact, for them, not having the children did in fact allow them to focus more time on each other rather than raising children. And Ann and James could see this was in fact beneficial not having children since their couple friends with children did not seem to be as romantically bonded as they were, sans kids. James considered it just too hard to grow up on Earth but for Ann, not having children had something to do with the genetically related health problems she carried. Neither Ann nor James felt incomplete without children, despite the friends and parents often telling them they should have children.

Both Ann and James would often say in unison, "Why should be mess with something that already works so good?" And so, they did not, and a euphoric love kept them strongly bonded as a couple!

CHAPTER NINE

ATTAINING MORE SPIRITUAL KNOWLEDGE AND LIVING A LIFE REAL FINE AND THEN WATCHING THINGS COME TO A GRIND!

WHAT HAPPENED AS a result of the spiritual, esoteric and scientific knowledge Ann and James assimilated was nothing short of astonishing growth. With it came a much broader perspective of things and an increased ability to deal with problems and also to be more creative from the perspective of artistic pursuits and music. It gave access to greater healing power for themselves and others. But what really piqued both Ann and James interest was a group Ann found out about, called the Tibetan Foundation!

This was another of those things Ann found in her incessant search to learn more. The group was based on the Theosophist teachings of such esoteric luminaries as H.P. Ledbetter, Madame Blavatsky, Annie Bessant, Rudolph

Steiner, and Alice Bailey. Specifically, it was based on most closely on the many books written by Alice Bailey which she transcribed through a spiritual channel, Dwal Khul, an ascended Tibetan master. Although Alice Bailey was already deceased, another channel, Janet McSure, began channeling Dwal Khul and was doing so in public.

It was in the Crystal Cave Bookstore that Ann and James had the opportunity to hear Janet McSure channel her messages from Dwal Khul and it seemed to them the messages being shared with them had many insights into spiritual matters involving past lifetimes, the spiritual planes (including the heavenly realms) and how to live in these higher dimensions while on Earth and to serve humanity so as to create a Heaven on Earth, with the sharing of this with humanity as the focus. This idea of serving humanity appealed immensely to both Ann and James.

By viewing what people resonate with, you get an insight into their spiritual enlightenment. And for sure Ann was excited by being involved in a project to uplift humanity. She queried James about this, "James, are you excited about a project that would make things better on Earth?"

"Duh", James replied, "What could be more important than that? I have been looking like something like this since I was five years old!" "I agree,"

Ann exclaimed, "we should really pursue this and see where it leads, I can see you agree, James!"

An Angel Not Perceived
Dr. Robert J. Newton

Hearing all of this brought Ann a reawakening of knowledge so utilized while in the highest dimensions of Heaven. And once such knowledge is resurrected, it allows a person to live with more understanding and with a real purpose in life, on fast track. So, as Ann assimilated her new awareness, she was most effusive and shared this knowledge with her parents, her friends and co-workers and yet none of them were interested in these things, save James. The problem Ann and James had in sharing this insightful and useful information was it being too far removed from the existing belief systems of people, especially Christians, Moslems and Jews.

People such as Buddhists and Hindus could actually comprehend and accept what Ann and James were learning but neither of them associated with these faiths, so they were limited to their knowledge and the other people involved with and following the Tibetan Foundation. This ultimately worked in their favor as it takes a special and devoted person to understand things outside of the mainstream belief system.

The concept of the Tibetan Foundation was for people to become infused with spiritual knowledge and then apply it so there was a more equal distribution of resources and wealth. Today this would be called Zeitgeist as promoted by associated groups such as the Thrive organization and Michael Tellinger's Ubuntu organization, but this was the middle 1980's and much before such concepts were seriously considered. The ultimate evolution was supposed to occur by people teaching other people high spiritual precepts so as to create something akin to a heaven on Earth. Ann and James found a renewed passion, not only teaching other people the Tibetan Foundation interacted with, but also learning to channel entities from other spiritual dimensions, including but not limited to Dwal Kuhl, who was also channeled by Janet McSure.

The couple worked hard to become Certified Channels of the Tibetan Foundation…learning to channel information at an accuracy level of 85% or higher. Other channels were certified within the same parameters. At first there were few problems associated with the practice but as more channels started being certified and channeling in public, there were contradictions in the information being accessed by the various channels. The conflicting data created an interesting atmosphere of doubt about something that was supposed to be certain. The question remained whether confidence or comfort were found in the Head Channel, Janet, who was the arbiter of what was most accurate and what was not!

If this was not enough to get the "boat rocking," and making things unstable, the Tibetan Foundation, via the channeling of Janet McSure, had created a way to cleanse the mind of defects and destructive emotions and reprogram the human mind to a more optimal level of functioning. At least that was the idea of what this "pattern clearing/mind clearing" technique was supposed to achieve and yet things seemed to not lead to more harmonious results for the individuals and couples who used this approach. In fact, just the opposite occurred.

An Angel Not Perceived

Dr. Robert J. Newton

For Ann, the general discord manifested into a mental and emotional state of uneasiness, unlike the normal state of tranquility she always conveyed. It got to the point where Ann decided she must halt her involvement with the Tibetan Foundation so she could re-attain a state of equilibrium. James on the other hand, chose to stay with the "rocking boat" that was listing so much as to be close to capsizing. Ann was much better than James at balance and decision-making. She knew when something was not functioning in her life and acted to remedy that. In fact, that had been her standard operating procedure since attending the Catholic Convent high school.

James, ever the optimist, considered things as still being salvageable and continued to spend a lot of time trying to get the Tibetan Foundation out to the public at large. But he was not ready for the test he would face soon after Ann's departure from the Tibetan Foundation. He spent too much time in the foundation and virtually no free time with Ann. And, as Shakespeare explained it, it is interesting how people who are deeply in love can get pulled apart by "the slings and arrows of outrageous fortune." This is in fact what happened to James, when he met the alluring Michelle, who was also involved in the Tibetan Foundation.

Rather than spend his time with Ann, James began to spend time with Michelle— who put out all the signals that she "was available." Ann was the only woman with whom James had been intimate with; she was a most alluring and beautiful woman herself. Yet James could not resist Michelle, since she was into the same cause as himself, and just exuded sexuality and sensuality like nothing he had experienced before. One could say it was inevitable that James became sexually involved with Michelle—confused by his changing thoughts about Ann and unable to resist Michelle's allure.

Ann sensed something was going on with James and he might be "cheating" on her. He spent virtually no time with her and was off to work early in the morning and then off to the Tibetan Foundation in the evening, often into the wee hours of the night. Before too long, Michelle wanted a commitment from James, which he found extremely difficult while still married to Ann. It was even more difficult for James to even talk to Ann about getting a divorce. First, and foremost, she had never wronged him in any way, shape or form. Ann was never unfaithful, she never disrespected him and supported him in any way she could. Unfortunately, when Ann left the influence of the Tibetan Foundation, it ceased being one of her support functions.

Eventually, James broached the divorce issue with Ann, although he found it the most difficult thing he had ever done, including being in the Army and the combat missions he undertook. He basically told Ann he had found another woman in the Tibetan Foundation and he wanted a divorce so he and Michelle could be together. Ann asked him, "Why do you continue to be involved in the Foundation? Do you really think it serves your higher purpose?"

"Well", James replied, "Michelle and I think there is still a lot of value in the Tibetan Foundation! Certainly, there are at least two huge problems therein. Yet I believe in the long run we can do some amazing things there that will change the course of humanity, much for the better!"

"That is quite a rosy picture you paint there, James," Ann responded. "It is like a 'warzone' in the Foundation. Not only has our relationship been destroyed by the misperceptions therein, several other couples' relationships are a casualty thereof, also! If you would agree to leave the Foundation, I think our relationship can and will recover. But if you stay your course, our future is bleak and will actually be destroyed!"

"Well, I still disagree with you," James replied, "and I will continue in the Tibetan Foundation indefinitely!" Although a part of James knew that Ann's assessment of the Tibetan Foundation was correct, he could not bring himself to fully embrace that reality. It was too much of an adjustment for his subconscious mind to make! James was also ignoring the fact that Ann would be put in a precarious financial position. Most likely he was thinking with his "little head-brain" rather than his heart.

Nevertheless, Ann granted James the divorce he wanted, in the classy manner in which Angels do things. Whether James deserved such kind treatment is highly debatable but that is how things worked out. And yet just around the corner James found situations and scenarios where his hasty decisions would come back to haunt him.

The first surprise was how incredibly more the Tibetan Foundation became a center of conflict rather than a place of peace and enlightenment. There were personal rivalries and illegal decisions being made by the board of directors. James and his friend Slayton experienced personal attacks…a major channel calling them anti-Christ's. All of a sudden, James began to see the dysfunction within the foundation just as Ann had perceived. His modified perception made James realize just how askew and off-kilter things were becoming in the Tibetan Foundation. Additionally, Michelle got rather squirrely in her commitment to James and he was soon to find that she did not possess the kind of loyalty that was an innate part of Ann, and also was having a concurrent affair with another woman.

James was to discover how some things come back to "bite you in the ass," Regardless of his new awakenings, James was divorced and less financially secure than before since he gave Ann considerably more than half of the community property and assets they had amassed. in a multiplicity of ways. It was then James realized very painfully that divorcing Ann was an incredibly bad decision. But since he had made his decision, James knew he needed to play out the circumstances he had set in motion.

James, not one to embrace life alone would meet yet another woman while on the rebound from Michelle—who seemed incapable and/or unwilling to commit to marriage. In a moment of quiet, personal repose, James thought, *regardless how alluring and sexy Michelle is, I'd never had to face something like this with Ann.*

An Angel Not Perceived
Dr. Robert J. Newton

In short order, James married Penelope as his rebound wife. She was in a rush to commit and James was aware he was marrying into her many addictions and malfunctions. This man of valor believed he could get her on a drug and alcohol-free track, despite the odds of this occurring were so minuscule. The marriage was short-lived but produced one son...he would later reflect everything was doomed from the start, even though sure he could help his second wife.

This story must move forward with less about James and more about the Angelic Ann. It is hard to understand how such a beautiful, sweet and intelligent Ann would have so much difficulty finding another man to round out her life. Quite possibly...because the presence of an exalted Angel is intimidating to the greater majority of men. This would seem the only rational explanation. Rarely—only once in a great while—would Ann have a date with a man, with nary a spark felt by either of the two people involved, which was hard to believe, considering Ann's alluring beauty and feminine manner.

Beyond that, although James gave Ann about three-fourths of the marital estate in their divorce, financially, things were sketchy for Ann. Finances became even more stressful when her boss of many years closed his men's clothing store and Ann could only find minimum wage jobs in sales in women's retail clothing. Although her mortgage was much less than renting something comparable, the grind to make ends meet each month created a tremendous amount of stress, which ultimately resulted in some serious physical implications for Ann.

An Angel Not Perceived
Dr. Robert J. Newton

We must remember...Ann had incarnated with genetic defects including a weak liver, kidney, pancreas, and acute menstrual problems. Despite her more evolved Angelic origins, any stress of any sort always had major health implications for her. Her family was not close enough to help her—and seemingly kept their distance —by design. Part of this choice to distance themselves was predicated by the fact Ann was always on the cutting edge of things; her family could never relate to her beliefs, nor could they accept it or understand them! Ann did not have the fortune to exist in a culture, such as that of Hispanic communities where one more frequently finds active and caring extended families.

As was Ann's nature, rather than complain, in her Angelic state, she approached these changes in her life with an un-human like dynamic. The choice being made, Ann steeped herself in deepening spiritual and esoteric studies, which expanded into Yoga and Hinduism. They were just natural extensions of previous lifetimes Ann had spent in India. In the late eighties, very few people even knew about these beliefs, let alone pursued and practiced them! As he quietly watched her journey, James often thought, *the world at large not knowing something was never an impediment or obstacle would stop most left-handed people. And, that is my Ann!*

Things also changed in a major way in James' life and he had much to consider. He had a son with his second wife; his always challenging marriage was coming to an end. Two small items in life held such significance! James did not want to abandon the farm he developed in Virginia or be separated from his son, yet the writing was on the wall—he might be better off living back in California again. As he considered his choices, he thought, *What the hell! I really have no say in this matter anyway. My wife is divorcing me and taking my son to another state. Yet, hope still springs eternal—I may have some remote chance to reunite with Ann...my beautiful former wife and the most important of all my spiritual teacher and mentor.*

From this renewed perspective, James felt nothing could be better than living with an Angel and having this Angel possibly resume being his "master teacher." When James' farm was sold, he packed up his remaining possessions and once again drove the great span between Virginia and southern California. James had visited several times with Ann—when he would make his summer vacation trek back to California, even one time with his young son, Robert. He was hopeful because of those visits; they'd had some amiable interaction. Ann, however, was clueless James was moving back to California and so when he arrived at her doorstep, unannounced, she was pleasantly surprised to see her soul mate/twin flame, again!

Ann had always felt she and James should never have dissolved their relationship; she had only acquiesced in the end because it was what James wanted. When she saw him standing there a memory flashed through her mind, *Ah, James! He always got what he wanted—yet had to contend with realizing it wasn't working out anywhere near what he envisioned. I guess we have to accept how often this happens to other people in similar situations. Here I stand. Do I immediately banish James from my doorstep? Or do I give him hope there is perhaps some small chance for us to have a permanent reunion?*

Sensing something going on in Ann's mind, James felt his best plan was to speak candidly with her. "I know when I left you behind how wrong I was; you did not deserve that in any way, shape or form. I beg your forgiveness and ask that you pardon me for my indiscretions, Ann. I would very much like to reunite our energies, again!"

"I am so glad you are back here again, James, and to know you are no longer encumbered with another romantic relationship. In the end, we are all responsible for what we create in our lives. Blaming other people for what happens to us is not productive and I can see by the look in your eyes that you still love me immensely. So, whatever you did in the past is just that...the past!" James' felt his heart warm, as much by the playful smile in her eyes, as by what he next heard. "I would really like to have you at least as my boyfriend—if in fact you would want me as your girlfriend!"

"I would in fact like that so very much. It kind of blows me away that you would even give me a second or even third glance," James exclaimed. "For sure, I think we can go to a much deeper spiritual level than we did before. I am here because what we had previously was amazing, Ann, even considering the confusion and chaos stirred up by the Tibetan Foundation. I guess these are my cues, like 'Mr. Ooh's'— to take you out for dinner so I will not be considered a sinner," James chimed in his indomitable fashion!

70

An Angel Not Perceived

Dr. Robert J. Newton

James smiled as Ann just rolled her eyes and replied, "I so missed your humor, and that is not a rumor, and the way you turn a phrase, is nothing like a malaise. Yes, you hurt me, as much as could be done to your one and only Angel, you really let me dangle. Yet with you here now, I know how I feel, and it is like wow and pow!"

A new chapter began as these soul mates/twin flames reunited, and whilst there remained many great differences between them in personality and style, any other great things were magically rekindled that night at Mother's Market Restaurant, in Huntington Beach, California.

Ann told James, "I've thought about you many times, and yet...I never allowed myself to seriously hope we would be reunited romantically. You really have been the only one who 'got me'. Certainly, my parents never did nor did my sisters and brother. History reveals my previous boyfriends never had a clue, either. Even in the highest realms of heaven I never met anyone as amazing as you, my man of star origins!"

"You know I have never claimed to be as cultured or as fine a vibration as you, Ann. I have, however, thought of you a lot and realized very quickly that leaving you was a real dumb ass move on my part. Many synchronicities revealed that to me as the same similar events kept happening to me over and over again...well, my nose kind of got rubbed in it! To our many detractors, who felt we are mismatch and misappropriate as a couple, I just say, 'TFS, just eat your hearts out because you never had what we did, and you would be blessed if you ever did.' Ann, I must tell you, that you are the only reason I came back to this crowded mess in Southern California from my bucolic farm in Virginia!

CHAPTER TEN

THE CHANCE FOR ANN
TO MOVE FORWARD AGAIN!

WHILE ANN LIVED alone, and sans any other romantic relationship, she found herself so focused on mere survival her spiritual studies and the progress commensurate with it were significantly curtailed. Not only was Ann sick much of the time, she was being psychically attacked at night by dark astral entities. These dark entities could best be described as bad ghost or evil spirits who harassed someone while they were trying to sleep. The nocturnal visits complicated Ann's health even more—the lack of sleep she got during these "attacks" further diminished her health. Ann's visiting evil spirits exhibited no physical bodies, but they had the ability to use their energy to touch her, draining her energy from her neck or medulla oblongata, also known as the Alta-major, at the soft spot in the back of her head. Essentially, they functioned as energy vampires!

An Angel Not Perceived

Dr. Robert J. Newton

Once reunited, and in the beginning when Ann and James spent time together with each other only on the weekends, he invested considerable time chasing away the evil spirits that attacked her at night. He bravely amassed a significant amount of his own energy as well as any other energy he could channel from the realms of Heaven and other high dimensions. When Ann was alone, she would often sleep with the lights on in her bedroom in a bold stand to keep the evil spirits at bay.

Ann valued having James around to provide a strong support system that allowed Ann to re-pursue her intense search for the widening spiritual knowledge she was then able to incorporate into her life. She began a dedicated and intense study of Kriya Kundalini Yoga as taught in the lessons at Self Realization Fellowship, which was founded by Yogi Paramahansa Yogananda. James had studied a generic Yoga, during the late eighties but Ann's foray now—almost a decade later—was much deeper than anything James had previously experienced. Ann was gracious and eager to share her knowledge with James, from which he benefitted considerably, especially in regard to his temperament, which could be mercurial at times!

After two years from their initial reunion, James moved in with Ann. Her company was being moved to Los Angeles and she really was not up to the grind of commuting to work every day, from Santa Ana. She knew the additional stress would adversely affect her health, which she was grateful had improved considerably after James came back into her life. However, just before the move, Ann went to New York

City with her boss and his wife, to see the attractions of the town.

Ann was surprised at James' response when she asked him to accompany her. He told her, in no uncertain terms, "I am committed to several contracts for landscaping jobs, so I really cannot go. And even if I had the time, I have already been to NYC several times and really see no reason to go there again. The energy there is so confused and conflicted it does little more than create an overarching, disharmonious living atmosphere."

Her surprise was assuaged somewhat by the time she returned from NYC. She voiced her new-found agreement with James, stating, "I really could have really lived quite well without visiting 'The Big Apple'. It is more really like a big rotten Apple with too many people living in too small an area."

"Well, I told you much the same thing before you went to NYC, Ann. I have often felt I saw much more order in Cairo, Egypt than New York City. The confused energies there are just too skewed for anyone to live in a state of coherence or to attain a high spiritual perception and presence for almost everyone who lives there. There is a lot of electromagnetic pollution which interferes with and diminishes the energies of God/life force/Prana/Chi"

"I cannot disagree with anything you have said, James," Ann stated, "but let us focus on us and get our household established, since I am overjoyed we are living together now.

There are a couple of things I would love to do with you. The first thing I want is for us to learn Kriya Kundalini Yoga from Yogi Govindan, of Babaji's Kriya Yoga. I have been doing a lot of research on Govindan and he has dedicated his entire life to teaching Babaji's Kriya Yoga with a singular purpose and passion! I can assure you, James, you will learn a lot about Kundalini."

"Kundalini, shumundalini! You know I am already a master of Kundalini," James exclaimed. I have mastered this through the Tai Chi Standing Meditation and have had quite a few Kundalini energy awakenings. So, I doubt there is much I can learn from Yogi Govindan!"

"I know you know a lot about Kundalini, but you might want to consider how much more there is still for you to learn," Ann replied. "And if that is not enough, you would do me a huge favor by driving me to this weekend class."

"Well, since you put it like that, I guess I do not have a lot of choice, unless of course, I want to appear to be an uncaring and inconsiderate ogre!"

James should have known, given his past with Ann that he would ultimately go to the Kriya Kundalini Yoga class in Marina del Rey, California and once again...that Ann was in fact correct in her assessment of what Yogi Govindan was teaching. It is undeniable that James had experienced the very rare Kundalini experience, multiple times. Yet as he engaged in one of the meditations being practiced by the class, not only did he have an intense Kundalini experience, but he also went into Samadhi, wherein a person's breathing is spontaneously curtailed and the heart stops beating. This not only surprised James because he really hadn't initially considered that Kriya Kundalini Yoga had anything to teach him—it also amazed Yogi Govindan who specifically asked James, "Were you in Samadhi?"

Pause, James. Think now. How do you best respond when you know your consciousness is at least in the fifth dimension? James freely accepted the response that came to mind: *The truth, James. Always, the truth!* "Yes, I was in Samadhi, concurrent with a Kundalini awakening, Govindan!"

James' experience with Kundalini and Samadhi enabled him to acknowledge he would have to perpetually keep his mind open and pliable so as not to miss or possibly shun things that could be of great value to him.

Ann chided James somewhat when she exclaimed," I guess you didn't know everything about Kundalini, as you recently claimed. But what you did also surprised the class and Yogi Govindan and me too! You will need to share this experience with me, likewise, Mr. Smarty Pants! Sponge Bob called and wants his square pants back!"

Laughing hilariously, James mockingly replied, "That may be, but my pants aren't square although they be smart!"

"Aside from the wants of Sponge Bob," James replied. "I am very sure I have done this Kundalini and Samadhi gig many times in many past lifetimes in India. But I must tell you, Ann, Kundalini is as intense and extreme an experience as anyone can endure. Your face feels like it is burning up, there is an intense amount of life force/Prana/electrical energy coursing up and down your spine and you are completely disoriented—not really able to function in the third dimension since you are more than likely in the fifth or sixth dimension. How this happens I am not certain but that it does happen is a reality. So, my advice...be careful what you wish for and make sure you are prepared for such an insanely intense event!"

"So, you think Kundalini is beyond the purview of an Angel? In fact, in the highest dimensions of Heaven, from whence I came to incarnate on Earth, we live in a state of perpetual Kundalini, or something close thereto."

"I am well aware of that," James responded, "yet the whole Kundalini experience on Earth puts tremendous strain on the human body. And considering your menstrual issues, liver, heart and blood sugar swings, I feel compelled to alert you about what might transpire. Some people have also been considered to become afflicted by severe mental issues and sometimes a state of insanity...all from their Kundalini awakening. For you, Ann, I am more concerned with the physical stress rather than your being mentally diminished."

"I know you only have my best interests at heart!" Ann declared. "You are most likely right!"

So aside from the need to be aware and cautious, both Ann and James devoted themselves to a twice-daily practice of the major Kriya Kundalini Yoga protocols, including Asanas (stretching and counter stretching), Kriya Dhyana Meditations (controlled meditations) and Pranayam (extended breathing meditations). Ann's ultimate devotion and discipline to the activities exceeded that of James. One great benefit she experienced from her engagement was a major enhancement of the psychic abilities she gained. Ann became very proficient in telepathy (communicating with someone without verbalized words), remote viewing (seeing into the past or the future), clairvoyance (discerning things about people without any foreknowledge thereof), clairaudience (hearing things beyond the range of human perception) and clairsentience (figuring things out by feeling them).

James also developed these psychic abilities and both he and Ann could "read" each other so well they could not lie or deceive the other. The couple discussed being able to "read" people's thoughts and recognized the great advantage of being attuned to whether the truth was being told! However, they each also mentioned how great was the annoyance—the insult to one's intelligence when someone tries to put something over on you, and you know exactly what their deceit is.

Ann handled the "truth" issue far better than James; Angel's really do not let themselves be overly upset about anything. They choose instead to focus on expressing their divine nature of Love! Of course, Ann never claimed special positions from herself and would routinely acknowledge her belief that everyone could express divine qualities. She would even tell James very often, "Oh James, you are quite Angelic yourself. You just haven't seen it yet!"

Another item on Ann's bucket list was to go to Hawaii again and with James. Her previous trip had been with her sister when Ann and James were discussing a divorce. James was excited about going and shared with Ann all the places they could visit on Maui. As well as Ann, James was quite enthralled by the *love energy* that seemed to ooze from every part of the island. While James shared, Ann thought, *this could just be the vacation where we can become more closely bonded…melded…and experience a deeper connection. I hold so much hope that one day, someday, we can become less individual and more cohesive.*

The vacation turned into a shared event—with Ann's younger sister, her brother in law and their young daughter. Ann cherished the time with James. It was important to her because she harbored the fear she would not live past the age of fifty and she was already forty-four. James expressed his desire to get into the water at least once at Lahaina or Maalaea to go surfing while there, yet he seemed more excited to go up the Hana Coast to explore the many secluded beaches along the way to Hana and Seven Sisters, a river with deep pools of water. He reminded Ann, "there are few places on Earth as lush as this north shore of Maui. Here, surrounded by land, lushly covered with coconut palms, ferns, fruit trees, and other tropical plants and grasses, we are reminded they are all attributed to the large amount of rain that falls in this area and the rain, which also contributes to the many beautiful waterfalls in the area."

The happy travelers also partook of the amazingly beautiful black sand beaches. Surrounded by all the beauty, Ann found herself immersed in a heavenly landscape that transported her back to the highest dimensions of heaven. She was incredibly grateful to have James show her the myriad points of interest and entertain her as a personal tour guide. Ann, thinking how amazing to have fruit stands in Hana, where they bought mangoes, coconuts, papayas, strawberry bananas, and pineapples, smiled and told James, "This fruit will make a most delicious lunch. What if we let it titillate our pallets and head up the coast?" James smiled and nodded in agreement, as he smacked his lips. Quiet overtook the interior of the car...each relishing the tasty fruit.

When they finally got to the Seven Sister's Pools, past Hana, Ann spotted some dolphins in the ocean. Becoming unusually animated she explained to James, "You know, James, the dolphins are the most evolved creations on Earth. Even in the highest realms of heaven, there are dolphins and they are respected and revered—by virtually who has attained that level. I know, this is in great contradistinction to Earth where we experience that people like dolphins but have no real understanding of how divine they really are. I wonder if any of the people around us really get it. I know you do, James, because you surf with them and are always raving about their magnificence, but I really do wonder about the majority of others who limit their experience with these beautiful creatures."

81

"Well," James exclaimed, "the more time you spend around these evolved beings the more you appreciate them. And the way they navigate with ease around the ocean is something to behold! They will pop up from under the water right next to me and scare the shit out of me. They once scared me so much, I fell off my surfboard when I was riding a wave. But in essence, I do understand they are only playful and not mean. They really don't know how to be mean or less than loving, even when they've been trained by the U.S. Navy to deliver torpedoes as weapons."

"Well we are not here to weaponize Maui, James, but instead, to feel the love that seems to permeate everything.," Ann declared with an intense sincerity. "This place is probably as close to Heaven as there is on Earth… not the citified spots, but the rural areas, the jungle areas…even the ocean!"

"I agree and then some," James replied in an authoritative fashion, "and doesn't this make you want to meditate and see what else we can tune into?"

"You must have been reading my mind," Ann declared. "There is no better way we could spend our time!"

Ann and James took their time enjoying what crossed their paths as they navigated their way over to a big rock along the river edge at one of the Seven Sisters Pools. The place seemed to capture their attention…their spirits. It seemed just and fitting to sit down on the rock and cross their legs into the Lotus meditation position. Since they were serious, world-class meditators, both could descend into a deep meditative state with little effort. In fact, they spent much of their waking hours in a meditative trance of sort. But oh! The power of the ocean! The negative ions being released by the crashing water of the river and the breaking waves created a negative ion-rich environment that was extremely conducive to meditative states in the brainwave levels, particularly of lower theta and upper delta.

Irrespective of the difficulties involved to describe a deep meditative experience, suffice it to say that Ann and James were able to enter a transcendent state, surpassing anything possible on Earth. When very deep brainwaves are accessed by a person, it not only allows access to higher dimension, including Heaven, it also allows someone to project their consciousness to a whole different place and to the dimensions of bliss which are rarely perceived on Earth. Few people on earth have been made aware of this depth of meditation. But as you might expect, Ann, being inherently Angelic, was James' teacher about transcendent states of consciousness.

These transcendent/liberating brainwaves are accessed by Tibetan monks and Indian Yogis that inhabit monasteries in India and Tibet and elsewhere. Ann often referred to these deep meditative states as the doorway and path to the "divine realms of God." When in these exalted realms, Ann would often remind James, "You know these meditative states are what allow us to access the 'cosmic internet' and what is referred to as *Akashic knowledge*...heavenly records. And, of course, you know James, that Satguru Patanjali in *The*

83

Yoga Sutras, referred to this same thing as Celestial Hearing—accessing knowledge stored in the Heavens."

"Yes," of course James replied, "you have exposed me to all of this or perhaps I should more accurately say…re-exposed me to things from my past incarnations on Earth. In the Hindu *Vedas,* this is called Akashic knowledge, which is knowledge stored and accessed in the skies. Also remember further, in Dr. Hurtak's book, *The Keys of Enoch,* he wrote about there being a huge computer in the center of the Universe where all knowledge that has ever existed is stored and can be retrieved.

"For sure," Ann exclaimed. Her voice held a lot of force and her face, a wry smile, "I'm sure you remember, too, how mind blowing and hard to assimilate this concept was the first time you were exposed to this idea."

"For sure, that is an understatement," James exclaimed, with a broad smile on his face." It took me several years to really, chew, swallow and digest that whole giant computer idea."

"And yet when you realize that human DNA is a binary pairs computer code, this idea does not seem so bizzaro, and maybe I can get a *cigaro,*" James continued in a gleeful manner!

"Dr. Huert Yockey talks about the DNA computer codes in his book, *Information Theory, Evolution, and the Origins of Life.* Even Bill Gates described our DNA as a very complex binary pair computer code, more complex than anything ever written by Microsoft Corp. I would not be surprised if all of creation is based on computer codes—not only animate things but inanimate objects, likewise."

"Certainly, although I would like to stay here tonight and talk about this, much more," Ann opined, "I'd guess my sister and brother-in-law are expecting us back tonight. And, since the Sun has already set, I guess we should return. We can certainly talk more about computers, DNA and creation on our way back and anything else that pops into your creative mind, James."

Thus, with James at the wheel and with the Moon making its presence felt, the glorious golden disc shimmered on the Ocean!

The ride back allowed Ann to concentrate on the Moon and the Ocean and to bask in the magical presence of the sublime moonbeams. For her, there was certainly no more sublime a way to end a day than this. James could feel the effects of this but really had to concentrate on driving back on the narrow and winding road along the Hana Coast. "Ann expressed her gratitude to James on the drive back when emoted, "James, thank you so much for you driving on this twisting road and allowing me to bask in the wonders of the Moon. You know I hate driving on narrow twisty roads, anyway."

"You are a real funny bunny, Ann," James laughingly replied, "since you don't even like being a passenger on a twisty road, and since it also reminds you too much of the Mr. Toad ride at Disneyland, I took you on long ago, back in the late sixties."

"Yeah, James, you really sold me a bill of baloney on that one, promising the ride was tame, which was lame and insane," Ann mockingly replied.

So, when they got back to their hotel in Kihei, Ann's sister said, "I thought you guys had left the planet or something because we thought you were coming back much sooner than you did."

"Ann replied, as a matter of fact, "Well we did leave the planet in a manner of speaking and we might not really be back yet anyway, even though we are here."

"What do you mean by that?" Ann's sister queried.

"No disrespect intended but I really do not want to become distended" Ann replied, "and it would be hard to tell you in words you might understand. Suffice to say we were transported to another world today, especially after our intense meditation at The Seven Sister's Pools and then driving back in the sublime effects of the moonlight." James just loudly laughed, rolled his eyes and nodded in agreement with what Ann had conveyed! "Some... actually a lot, of magic happened today, "James exclaimed.

"When we went with you guys to Honolua Bay," Ann explained, "it was really cool, but this was beyond... a real magical mystery tour, *du jour*!"

CHAPTER ELEVEN

AND REMAINING IN A STATE OF HEAVEN WITH MORE LEAVEN ON EARTH

A WEEK OF time for a vacation on Maui is in fact a short duration, especially when you factor in the travel time involved. Ann and James talked about how grateful they were to get the small yet wonderful taste of paradise on Maui. Ann was taking a lot in, and soon realized that no matter where one happened to be, it was possible to live in a state of heaven on Earth.

Ann harkened back to Mary Baker Eddy who had stated such in *Science and Health with Key to the Scripture,* where she wrote, "It is possible to live in a state of Heaven on Earth." Mrs. Eddy came to this and many other realizations after being sent home to die by her doctors—and yet— healed herself from a deep study of the Bible. In fact, from everything Ann and James had studied about Mrs. Eddy in all her writings, including the autobiographical ones, she appeared unperturbed by anyone or any situation. Even when she was attacked and insulted, Mrs. Eddy never held any animosity or resentment and even blessed her so-called enemies, and at the same time disarmed them. Additionally, Mrs. Eddy healed thousands of people!

The infamous woman seemed to always be happy, after she discovered "Christian Science." She never felt the need to belittle other people and consistently did the impossible, including raising people from the dead and building a huge church during World War I. She accomplished these things when during a serious shortage of materials and laborers, to create a magnificent edifice at the Mother Church, The First Church of Christ Scientist, in Boston, Massachusetts.

Of course, some people scoffed at the so-called "idiotic notion" that Mrs. Eddy harbored that she could build a world-class church in the circumstances of World War I, and yet in fact it was materialized and in a seemingly impossible time frame.

While Ann would not be confined just to Christian Science, as is evident from what transpired previously in her life, she certainly admired Mrs. Eddy as a teacher and model to emulate. Likewise, the earthly acknowledged leader of Kriya Kundalini Yoga, Babaji Nagaraj, was another powerful influence on Ann. While James focused on the extended breathing protocols of Kriya Kundalini Pranayam and the recitation of Sanskrit mantras (like rosaries) associated with Kriya Yoga, Ann focused on deep Kriya Dhyana meditation, studying all of Babaji Nagaraj's writings and those of the other Kriya Kundalini Yoga Masters, such as Thirumoolar, Valmiki, Konkanavar, Boganathar and Agastyar, but not limited thereto. Ann was also even more devoted to recitation of the Sanskrit mantras/prayers than was James, evidenced by the time she devoted to such.

Kriya Kundalini Yoga was a way for the couple to regenerate their bodies. Ann's genetically damaged body created constant limitations on what she could do, especially in regard to being vital and filled with energy. James, on the other hand, was always infused with a tremendous amount of Prana and the life force energy and vigor that comes therefrom. He fully understood that Yoga is about the union of the body and mind, and God and man, the root word being "Yug" or "Yog" means "union."

James also understood that Ann, in her Angelic wisdom, would naturally search out such a discipline and path. By following her intuition down the Kriya Yoga path, Ann did in fact extend her life beyond what she would otherwise have experienced without the knowledge and practices she culled therefrom—beyond the fifty years she thought she would not exceed.

As James saw just how much Ann was sustained by Kriya Kundalini Yoga, he grew increasingly more dedicated to the practice likewise. He intuitively knew Ann was extremely fragile and that her life in a body was very limiting, something she never experienced as an Angel in Heaven. He was also in constant awe of how Ann could be in such a good mood and how much she devoted herself to the study and practice of Kriya Kundalini Yoga and Hinduism. James knew full well that people of a much stouter constitution and better health would not be able to muster the focus and dedication to study, practice Yoga and recite thousands of mantra repetitions per day as he knew Ann engaged in, including the Gayatri Mantra, Krishna Mantra, Babaji Nagaraj Mantra and many others.

In fact, it could be said with one hundred percent assurance that Ann was more dedicated to practicing Kriya Kundalini Yoga and Hinduism more than almost any Indian citizen of the world, and at least as much as a Hindu Vedic Priest or any Indian Holy Person or Hindu Renunciate. It was as though while Ann knew it was possible to go into a state of physical immortality, such as Jesus and Babaji Nagaraj, she accepted the reality she would not be doing such and that her mission was to return to the highest realms of Heaven. On the other hand, she often encouraged James in his quest for physical immortality and she was equally impressed with James, seeing how he could go into a state of Samadhi, where he suspended his breath and heartbeat, for long periods of time during the day!

James was bothered to no end...knowing Ann would not be able or maybe was not even supposed to go into Soruba Samadhi—a constant state of physical immortality on Earth. So much so, in fact, he would often ask Ann, "Why do you not join this quest for physical immortality with me? Truly, this planet needs you to remain here even more than me, *mon ami!*"

90

An Angel Not Perceived

Dr. Robert J. Newton

Ann, saving her words, responded through mental telepathy, *you know, James, I truly love you and respect your attainments in Kriya Kundalini Yoga.. But there is a certain time frame from beyond which I was not supposed to exceed in my incarnation here. When I told you a few years ago, I would be lucky to exceed fifty years of age, it was because that was supposed to be the span of my incarnation here, and then I was supposed to return to the highest realms of Heaven...the Ninth Paradise...the ninth dimension, again. Yet when that time came in 1999, the White Brotherhood in the highest realms of Heaven, decided that I could have at least ten more years here, to try to finish or last complete more of my work.*

James responded telepathically in kind, *I have actually known that because I can read your thoughts, as you can read mine. I could most likely do so, even if we were not soul mates and twin flames. It is just that I have become so attached to you, romantically and as my teacher, and do not want our stint together to end! I would prefer us to go on into infinity, as we mesh together so well. But I guess relationships rarely, if ever, go on in an unbroken line into infinity!*

"Well you know that I know that you know," Ann continued aloud, in a state of certitude. "that the telepathic connection is unbroken when you realize there is no distance that can keep people from communicating and even rendezvousing with each other even when souls are separated by different dimensions. If you think about the way we met the first time in 1968 in this incarnation—was it not amazing how we both wanted to be with each other from our very first brief meeting at the Costa Mesa Christian

Science Church. That was not a chance meeting, James, but something we created at from remote locations in different dimensions. These kinds of things happen all the time and yet virtually no one is aware of it. Something tells me you are seeing it right now."

Ann continued, "What I am trying to share with you is we just need to let things flow as they will until it is my time to leave. My strong feeling is you will pull off the Soruba Samadhi gig because not only are you doing the things that make it possible through Kriya Kundalini Yoga Pranayam extended breathing meditation, and the other things you are doing but you are truly crazy enough to know you can achieve the state of physical immortality."

"Your vision and determination will serve you well and make your quest achievable, James. On top of that, I intuitively know we will reunite again after I go back to Heaven and you are down here in your immortal body of light and electromagnetic energy. In the meantime, you will be able to teach and instruct others how to experience immortality.

"Just imagine, James, the amount of wisdom and love that could be unleashed on planet Earth if you had a lot of other immortals living here. Truly it would unleash the prophesied 'Golden Age' of Earth, proclaimed by Krishna, 5,100 years ago, and as is prophesied in the *I Ching*, the Hopi prophesies and the Mayan prophesies. Seems to be a lot of overlapping confirmation here, no? Lest we ever forget Revelation 1:21, we have a confirmation of these other prophesies in the words, *and I saw a new heaven and a new earth, and the first earth were passed away....*"

CHAPTER TWELVE

RECEIVING HELP FROM A FRIENDLY ELF

SO, THE LEARNING, practices and wisdom kept flowing to Ann. While she and James were involved in a Kriya Kundalini Yoga meditation group, they met a couple, Mindy and Yar, with whom they really hit it off. They not only were in the same meditation groups but also enjoyed each other's company socially. Ann and James shared insights from their long-time practice of Kriya Yoga, since Mindy and Yar had only recently become involved in this discipline. In kind, Mindy, like an amazing friendly elf, shared with Ann an amazing esoteric knowledge from "The 72 Names of God," from Exodus 14, verses 19-21 of *The Torah*.

At first Ann studied the depth of these names by herself, but when James spied her perusing the list at her alter one morning after her morning meditation and mantra session, his curiosity got the best of him. "Just what is this you are studying?" James queried. "They appear to be in Hebrew, but how do you use them?"

"Well you are right James; they are in Hebrew but how did you know that?" Ann replied.

"I studied the *Aramaic Bible*, with Dr. Rocco Erico at The Church of Daily Living for a couple of years, so I have some experience in Hebrew."

"These *72 Names of God* are the hidden gem in the *Torah*. Ann replied. "They are not in the *Old Testament*...only *The Torah*. In fact, just like *Science and Health with Key to the Scripture*, which properly explains the *New Testament*, these *72 Names of God* explain all the aforementioned texts! Actually, they closely overlay *Science and Health*...in a hauntingly close synchronicity, at least from the perspective of explanation and understanding the nature of reality and the essence of God! Additionally, there are '72 Angels of God,' that correspond to the *72 Names of God*, and these cross-validate each other!"

"In that case," James exclaimed, "start laying this stuff on me. I am sure it is also going to mesh with Kriya Kundalini Yoga in some complementary fashion, as well."

"In fact, James, you are most likely correct because the seventh name of God, *Aleph Kaf Aleph*, means 'restoring things to their perfect state,' which is in fact the purpose and goal of Yoga (union with God). This union leads to a state of perfection. And the top line of the 72 Names is comprised of

8 Names that could be used in Christian Science healing treatments, as well."

"They are useful and beneficial beyond all measure. Just to let you know, James, *Achaiah,* the Seventh Angel of God, is associated with the sharing of wisdom and accomplishing hard tasks—like restoring things to perfection—maybe?"

"Ok, James, let's start with the first name of God." James glanced over and noticed Ann had an expression of intense focus on her face. "*Vav Hey Vav,* is fixing the past and creating happiness, and the First Angel of God is Vehuaiah, who also accomplishes difficult tasks—would not being happy make something like this more enjoyable to do—creating a state of happiness?"

"Are you ready to learn a few more, James? The second name of God, *Yod Lamed Yod,* means boosting your energy. The Second Angel of God is Jeliel, associated with victory over an attack, and would that not require boosted energy?. The third name, *Samesh Yod Tet,* references the making of miracles, and the Third Angel of God, Guardian Angel Sitael, is associated with miracles and protecting us from an attack. Would this knowledge be useful, Mr. Smarty Pants?"

"Yeah!" laughed James. "Mr. Smarty Pants—who is the friend of ants, and might even have them in his pants— concurs with your evaluation, Ann."

James watched Ann's laughter, thinking how it made her eyes sparkle. He also saw the visible change in her as she shifted to a serious mind and shared more information about the names they had been discussing. "The fourth name is, *Ayin Lamed Mem*, and denotes eliminating negative thoughts. The Fourth Angel of God, Elemiah, provides us relief from mental troubles, and this is appropriate and useful when we are dealing with negative thoughts...how could it not be? The fifth name is *Mem Hey Shin*, which is healing. The Fifth Angel of God is Mahasiah, who helps us live in peace, which is certainly a component of health and protection from disease... a lack of ease."

While in that highly focused state, James heard Ann suddenly exclaim, "The sixth name is *Lamed Lamed Hey*, which denotes understanding subconscious messages, and the Sixth Name of God is Lelafel. It is he, James, who helps us cure disease, using our subconscious abilities...our intuition... our inner knowing, from our subconscious mind, among other things!"

It seemed to James that Ann could not pull her eyes away from her chart on the names of God. He listened intently as she revealed more of her newly-discovered knowledge, and heard her voice soften as she revealed, "The seventh name is *Aleph Kaf Aleph*, which is restoring things to their perfect state, and associated with Anchaiah, who shares with us patience and learning—and the ability to perform hard tasks. The eighth name is *Kaf Hey Tav*, means eliminating negativity. The Eighth Angel of God is Cahetel, who is known to drive away evil and distracting spirits."

Ann giggled, the soft laughter that so often crept deep into James' heart, as she found a gentle balance between teaching and teasing him, "I am sure you will see this is very similar to what you might go through in the process of a Christian Science mental healing treatment, oh, James, of the most very smart pants!"

"In fact," James replied, "it is hauntingly similar to that! I wonder if anyone other than you or me really sees that. What you shared is so powerful and useful."

"So, what is recommended by the Kabbalah Center is that you repeat these namea once each day or even more," Ann relayed to James. "Furthermore, if we look at the "numbers," by taking the *72 Names of God*, with the "72 Angels of God," we get the sacred number of 144, which equals nine—the number of completion and God."

Ann picked up a touch of James being smug when he responded, "Well, I have already memorized the first line of the *72 Names of God*!"

"That is really groovy, Ann replied," but it would be even more meaningful, beneficial and powerful to learn to pronounce the names in Hebrew! Are you up for that Mr. Smarty Pants?"

"I wasn't until you threw down that challenge," James exclaimed, "but now it is game on!"

"You know you are pure putty in my hands, James," Ann laughed, passing imaginary putty, back and forth in her hands, "that is just what I wanted you to do. This is going to be delicious and duhlicious, as well"

"Haha, haha, LMAO," James replied as he mocked Ann, "but you did not have to manipulate me to get me to do something self-evidently beneficial for me, Ann. It certainly is not painful, like being burned in a hot frying pan!"

As James studied and learned to pronounce the myriad names, he found them to be a powerful tool in his life just as they were in Ann's. He directly incorporated the *72 Names of God* and the 72 Angels of God in the "Theta Healing" protocol treatments he used to heal patients. But beyond this, many other things were happening to Ann, as well as James. James started taking pulse oximeter readings of the oxygen saturation levels in Ann's body. He was confident the increase was represented by the Kriya Kundalini Yoga practices she was religiously undertaking—as well as the absorption of more molecular hydrogen, like H^2O_2 and H^3O_2, as revealed in the research of Dr. Gerald Pollack and his EZ Water.

While reviewing the new pulse oximeter readings, James considered the possibility of a correlation between The *72 Names of God* Ann was reciting, and even higher Oxygen saturation levels, which were being revealed. This would relate to better health from higher amounts of Prana/Chi/Life Force being carried throughout the body with the higher levels of oxygen and hydrogen, therein. This is in fact what James knew often happened for the Yogis and Yoginis who devoted themselves to the practice of Yoga, especially Kriya Kundalini Yoga. He also knew, in fact, very few people ever have the discipline to attain this blessed benefit in their lives...a discipline James knew he and Ann shared.

Ann had come to believe that both the protocols of meditative breathing of Kriya Kundalini Yoga and recitation of Sanskrit mantras—and on top of this—the recitation of The *72 Names of God* could in fact lead to a body that did not have to die...a body that could exist on Earth as long as the inhabitant of the body so desired! She paused for a few minutes, thinking about the possibility of immortality, *I know immortality is just not in the cards for me, but it could be for James! I also know he genuinely believes beyond doubt immortality is fact possible; I know he is grateful for every effort I extend to help him materialize such a scenario in his life.*

Both Ann and James knew for the Earth to materialize its destiny of *Aleph Kaf Aleph*—restoring things to their perfect state—there would need to be enough people living on Earth with greatly extended lifetimes so as to be able to share their wisdom and knowledge and leadership of how to do this. One foundation for Ann's belief, which James later embraced, was the extended lifetimes of Anunnaki, an extra-terrestrial race that first inhabited Earth about 450,000 years ago. The couple had read about the Anunnaki as was discussed in depth in several of Zecharia Sitchin's twelve books, including *When Time Began* and *The Twelfth Planet.*

Ann had figured out the extended lifetimes of 800-900 years in *The Old Testament* and *The Torah*, attributed to Moses and Methuselah and other figures, were actually Anunnaki, of extraterrestrial origin. This was supported by Sitchin's study of what is referred to as *The Sumerian Tablets*. So, Ann tried to figure out how the great knowledge in these tablets was kept from humanity for hundreds of thousands of years. The only concrete conclusion she could come to was the existence of people and religions who did not want these things to be even remotely considered by the populace at large through the intervening years of the Anunnaki...and the here and now!

Additionally, with the combined understanding about immortal lifetimes James and Ann shared from their study and practice of Kriya Kundalini Yoga, they shared the belief the ultimate purposes of Kriya Yoga, was attaining a union with God and immortalizing the human body—as opposed to a variant belief about dying and going to Heaven and then attaining the immortalized state. In the Kriya Yoga tradition Ann and James knew of the Kriya Kundalini Yoga Siddhas, masters of time, and space who had transcended death through the study and practices of Kriya Kundalini Yoga. This occurred as described in *The Yoga Sutras*, by Siddha Yogi Patanjali.

James spoke of this with Ann, one evening, to give his heart the solace that she understood the practices in the same context he did. "Ann, did you take the same thing from your reading, that as Patanjali related, first a Kriya Yoga initiate must master Kriya Dhyana or Kriya Dharana, which are structured meditations, which give the practitioner thereof the ability to control their mind? And, that what we know as Pranayam, or structured breathing meditations, must be mastered and the mastery of these things lead to Samadhi?

"I believe so, yes, James. As I understand it, Samadhi is first a temporary state where an initiate suspends their breathing and heartbeat, for varying periods of time. When they have mastered Samadhi at will, which is the ability to initiate it whenever and wherever, the exercise can lead to a state of Soruba Samadhi—wherein the body enters a state of super suspension and there is simply no need for breathing, hydration, or eating—and a body can be moved at will through all time and space as one's mind desires!"

Later, Ann would recall how James addressed this issue of various cultures in Dr. Newton's book, *Beyond the Mists of Time: When Trees Ruled the Earth*, wherein he went back in time beyond the acknowledged timelines of history and personally discovered the ancient Indians, Lemurians, Atlantians, Egyptians and Mayans, who in fact were aware of Soruba Samadhi, in one iteration or another. So, despite the fact virtually everyone thought the concept of physical immortality was sheer lunacy, Ann and James had gained significant evidence to the contrary, back into antiquity!

James was compelled to understand the particular groups who would not want this information within the circulation of humanity at large. In all he had read and was able to ascertain, the specific groups he was convinced would not want people to believe they could live immortally included the Roman Catholic Church and the other Christian Churches. To further pursue this line of reasoning, James had to consider, *what of the Zionists—a group and secular Jews and the Illuminati/deep state—should they not also be included in this collective? It isn't rocket science to recognize the power of these churches comes from parishioners who believe they are sinners who need to be saved and redeemed to have any chance of going to Heaven. I must not forget the Illuminati, controlling the worlds banking system, who control us by having control of monies of the multitude of countries, certainly would not want to lose their control of the world's money supply. So, there is plenty of blame to go around!*

Being honest with himself, James was confident he was not just picking on the Catholic or Protestant Churches; he was acutely aware, however, that other than Buddhism and Hinduism, none of the other churches really taught that man had any chance of immortality. "This all comes to mind...knowing that these two religions, both of which Ann has studied and practiced, still believe a person must reincarnate many times to achieve this state of immortality, enmeshed in a recurring cycle of birth and death."

Broaching this topic with Ann, she commented, "So again, even with these churches, you are still trapped in the illusion that many lifetimes are necessary to enter a state of union with God and get off the "Wheel of Karma." This is a travesty, James. While all the time *Aleph Kaf Aleph* reveals we are inherently perfect, which Jesus echoed when he declares in John 14:12 of the *New Testament*, "Verily, Verily, I say unto you, He that believeth on me, the works that I do shall he do also, and greater works than these shall he do…"

Based on Ann's response, James' mind wandered to some of the Kabbalists, a sect of Judaism, who held the belief that through "The Tree of Life" and the *72 Names of God* immortality of the physical body could be attained likewise. But certainly, in James' thoughts, this was such a small percentage of Judaism as to not even considered as realistic among mainstream Judaism.

Reading his mind, Ann said, "you know, James, the information and concepts are in this Kabbalistic approach, yet very few Rabbi's within this discipline even know the immortality gig is there!" Deep in her heart, Ann wanted him to focus on the possibility in the here and now, in this lifetime, where she believed existed the real possibility and actuality of suspending the state of death. She watched as James became fanatically focused on the concept they discussed so openly; she knew he believed anything less would end in failure, considering the negative thoughts of the mass consciousness of humanity which made achieving immortality just that much more difficult. They were both acutely aware of the ramifications, each having completed much research in the area of human thoughts affect what happens in the timeline/events that ultimately occur on Earth.

The seminal books the couple referenced on this subject were *The Hundredth Monkey*, by Ken Keyes, and *Morphic Resonance*, by Dr. Rupert Sheldrake. James commented to

Ann one day, "It is such strong, supporting evidence where these books discuss how the mass thoughts of humanity can create fields of energy that make some things possible and materialize and yet other things—not possible and not manifested."

All these discussions led Ann to further study *The Nature of Personal Reality*, by psychic channel, Jane Roberts. The information Jane shared in this book was that human thoughts can indeed affect what happens on Earth and even determine our weather and natural calamities...which led Ann to think, *this must also apply to human immortality!*

Then later, after digesting the manuscripts of Keyes, Sheldrake's' and Robert's books, Ann and James investigated how Quantum Mechanics also validated these points. Aside from the scientific evidence and channeled information in their books, the avid readers uncovered information from Quantum Physics. Imagine Ann's delight when James shared his understanding, "Another layer, Ann! We now have the classic experiment which also led Quantum researchers down the path that we can create our own reality/life. What a validation—that double slit experiment where researchers were able to affect the direction of beams of energy through using their thoughts!"

"I was equally excited, James, to see yet another valid point reveal that our thoughts create our reality. If you will also remember, as related to the aging process of humans, Dr. Ellen Langer did an experiment at Harvard University where she took septuagenarians and put them in a resort for two weeks without contact with the outside world."

"She saw that the participants were surrounded with a collection of pictures of themselves when they were much younger—and bombarded their minds with movies and TV and books and music and clothes from the fifties and sixties. After two weeks of this retro immersion, every participant had decreased wrinkles on their faces, had fewer aches and pains and felt younger and more energized; most actually looked younger than before the experiment."

The couple discussed at length the definite pattern of the possibility of immortality was being established. Beyond this growing pattern was other evidence being uncovered, which showed that as the telomerase strands at the end of DNA became longer, a person became healthier and with an extended lifetime and the opposite occurred as these strands became shorter. They could see the logic in the general belief among scientist's that it was inevitable the telomerase strands would become shorter and eventually a person would die. Yet James and Ann both held strong to all they discovered about the myriad possible steps to take, which could lengthen these strands, because they knew telomerase enzyme would continue to build these strands, which was produced as long as people smiled, laughed, danced, sang and meditated.

Ann responded well to her discipline in the extended breathing meditations in Kriya Kundalini Pranayama; the Sanskrit mantras, especially Aum, the Gayatri Mantra; and the Mahamrityunjaya Mantra. She found some pictures on the internet that showed how the cymatic force/vibrations from the "Aum Mantra" created geometric forms from the atomic level that could be photographed. And James found how the "Gayatri Mantra" and the "Aum" mantra, vibrationally—cymatically—created other geometric forms from the atomic level of creation which comprised the Indian Hindu mandala known as the "Shree Yantra."

Ann thought, *I also suspect that this same phenomenon, associated with the creation of atomic geometries, would also be manifested by what we know as the Mahamrityunjaya Mantra.* She was rather astonished, even with her Angel credentials, how everything was fitting together with the immortality quest which James was pursuing! She was elated and told James, "It will be exciting when you pull this off! You know I will be looking down on you from Heaven watching as things unfold. I know if anyone can pull this off it is you and I know you know it too, even though you never go about bragging about your abilities. So, don't let me down James, as this is really a co-venture!"

"You don't need to worry about my dedication, Ann, nor my resolve," James exclaimed, "I will not let you or myself down!" James then began to sing the Beatles song, *Don't Let me Down*, as his voice formed the song words.

Don't let me down, don't let me down, don't let me down, don't let me down.
Nobody ever loved me like she do me
Oh, she does
Yeah she does....

CHAPTER THIRTEEN

WEANING ONESELF FROM
THE CHAINS OF EARTH!

AT ONE POINT, Ann was visiting with Mindy, who shared with her a number of valuable lessons from the Builders of the Adytum (BOTA). This was something James was only tangentially involved with, but the things exposed to him he considered invaluable, as did Ann. The BOTA lessons were the culmination of all the substantial esoteric knowledge that was acquired and practiced by Dr. Paul Foster Case, who spent a considerable amount of time learning the knowledge of The Golden Dawn Rosicrucian's. He had worked himself up to a leadership position within the Golden Dawn yet became concerned because the grand leader of the group was practicing "white magic," which the learned Dr. Case considered as far too dangerous and foolish to dabble in, let alone seriously practice.

Reflecting on what he knew of Dr. Case, James stopped to remind Ann how Dr. Case had been focused on becoming a world class piano virtuoso and yet decided to leave the benefits of fame to follow the course of liberating and life-changing esoteric knowledge. Ann really didn't need James' reminder... all these things appealed to Ann so powerfully she was in awe of Dr. Case. This admiration led Ann and Mindy to study the BOTA lessons, which were a combination of many studies: the Rosicrucian teachings as well as Numerology, Astrology, Tarot, the *72 Names of God* from Exodus in *The Torah*, and *The Emerald Tablets* of Hermes Trismegistus.

Additionally, Ann found out that Dr. Case had also practiced Kriya Kundalini Yoga on his own and without a guru. Dr. Case said that was a mistake he regretted and commented that it was essential people be initiated into Kriya Yoga with the instruction of a Yogi/guru! This was probably one of the very few mistakes committed by the Amazing Case. As James listened to Ann, he knew, "with certainty, the system Dr. Case created with his disciplines placed him right smack at the top of the Pantheon of Esoteric/Spiritual knowledge!"

Following one of her conversations with James, Ann thought, *the way Dr. Case used his disciplines was in a manner they cross-verified each other, making the different disciplines far more understandable. This, in and of itself, appealed immensely to me but there are two things which Dr. Case created and translated I know to be the most concise and understandable spiritual treatises I've ever encountered.*

110

An Angel Not Perceived

Dr. Robert J. Newton

Dr. Case formulated *The Pattern on the Trestleboard: This is Truth About Self*, which were eleven statements of spiritual and scientific truth explaining the nature of creation and personal reality, one of which is, *From the exhaustless riches of its Limitless Substance, I draw all things needful, both spiritual and material.* After having become familiar with them, Ann thought, *anyone who studies these statements will be enriched and benefitted. I must make sure James studies them, too!*

The couple knew the esteemed Dr. Case had translated *The Emerald Tablets of Hermes Trismegistus.* They had read other translations of the *Emerald Tablets* yet none even came close to approaching the lyricism and insight as that of Dr. Case. In their minds, even the venerated Sir Isaac Newton didn't match Case's translation. Ann, with a combined value for Dr. Case's work, and the promises held therein was eager to voice her opinion. "James," she said, "You do realize the importance of this document is how it so clearly explains the perfect creation and how everything on Earth is interrelated, from the atomic level to the heavenly levels, and vice versa."

"Actually, Ann, yes, I do, James replied in a confident manner. "What I derived from my reading about this was the explanation of quantum physics and mechanics at least 2500 years before our venerated scientists of today. So, at a minimum, for at least 2500 years, the immortality gig could have been a reality in the Western World, aside from the knowledge held by those in India and China! You can see why everything Hermes hinted at is so incredibly exciting to both of us!"

An Angel Not Perceived
Dr. Robert J. Newton

Layer upon layer of wisdom, day after day, the couple found additional validation for their growing knowledge and beliefs. Ann discovered the personage of Hermes not only existed in Greece, but he was also in Egypt and Sumer as Thoth, as Tehuti in Atlantis, as Enoch in Israel, and in Meso America as Quetzalcoatl. In all the places Hermes inhabited, he was perceived as a person of great knowledge, abilities and understanding; everything Ann read reflected how he was venerated. She felt this great admiration gave added validation and weight to everything Hermes related in *The Emerald Tablets*. It also hinted that Hermes himself might well have achieved the immortality of the body she believed was possible. Hermes actually discussed this concept in another of his works, *The Corpus Hermeticum,* where he exhorts us to claim our right to be immortal beings. Ann then discovered the Arch Angel Michael had helped bestow this status of immortality on Enoch, as is related in *The Book of Enoch*.

Ann knew that her work was coming to an end on Earth…she began to see the culmination of her long search for the nature of reality…the nature of humans…and the potential for humans to exist in the same body in a state of immortality. She was vigilant in her pursuit and intention to not tell James of her status, yet he intuitively sensed it; this knowledge gave him a really crappy feeling. Yes, he had known it was inevitable, not because Ann could not attain immortality of her body but simply because it was time— and necessary for her to re-ascend to the highest levels of Heaven.

An Angel Not Perceived
Dr. Robert J. Newton

It was extremely difficult for James to watch how Ann's health steadily declined—especially so after having put all the pieces of the immortality puzzle together. Ann started bleeding daily due to a fibroid tumor, which had taken life within her uterus. Knowing how weak she was becoming Ann asked James to take her to the hospital to see if there was any way they could help her. Although he was reticent to do so, James did as Ann requested. However, the result was not what they had expected; her health was significantly worse...using the medicine prescribed!

Ann later acknowledged to James, "I guess you were right in not wanting to take me to the hospital since I have become very sick from the very medicines the doctors felt would benefit me. Before I went to the hospital, I was not throwing up; lately, I've thrown up several times a day for at least a week."

James didn't really want to pull the "I told you so" card, but he was frightened and frustrated. "That is exactly why I did not want you to go, Ann. Call it intuitive perception, if you will. I still have the hot pepper tincture I make and take myself and I just know it would stop the edema in your uterus!"

"I don't doubt what you are saying, James, yet we have had this discussion before about the hot pepper tincture. You know I can't stand the harshness of it; it creates a shock in my system I cannot tolerate."

"Yet the alternative," James replied, "is that you will bleed to death. So, I beg you to start taking a few drops of cayenne hot pepper tincture"

"Well that is not going to happen, either here on Earth or anywhere else!"

Subsequently, due to the continual loss of blood, the inability to keep down food or water, Ann became so weak she had become bedridden. She was so weak, in fact, James had to carry her to the bathroom. James lovingly stepped into the position of Ann's nurse...24/7. He knew in his heart it would be soon, too soon, before she re-ascended to the highest dimensions of Heaven. Thus, he was not surprised to hear her plaintive, "I am ready to go now James."

James struggled to keep his emotions in tow; Ann did not need the additional pressure, so he replied with something he felt was positive. "I know that, and I cannot understand how you are even still here since you have very little blood left in your body. You must be circulating Prana/life force in a way without using the circulation of blood. Physically you should be gone by now and yet here you are—still here!"

In a soft and weakened voice Ann asked, "Do you understand this, James?"

"I really do not," James replied, "other than you being between regular Samadhi and Soruba Samadhi—and yet we both know you are going to leave planet Earth through the normal death process."

An Angel Not Perceived
Dr. Robert J. Newton

This part of the couple's journey continued for two weeks as Ann's health diminished—and at three in the afternoon, when she collapsed on the toilet, they knew Ann was within her final hours. He had loved her gently and tenderly in those days, but seeing her in such pain and suffering, he wanted the woman he loved beyond all comprehensible words to be released. James ached when he placed Ann in the bed and saw her experience ever increasing severe pain. He fully understood the concept of being an empath—it was as though her pain was his own.

James was extremely discomforted in knowing Ann did not want him to embrace her. He understood it was because she did not want any attachments to Earth that would prevent her passing. Thoughts swirled around him, *I will always remember her strongly scolding me for trying to comfort our slowly dying cat, Arrow, when he was transitioning from Earth to Heaven. How she told me my loving intervention did little more than interfere with our pet's passing. This is a no-win situation and I know in my heart it will be a long time before I see any good in Ann's passing—other than her being released from pain and suffering.*

About two hours before she passed Ann interrupted James' quiet thinking and called out James' son, Robert, by name. James was heartbroken to tell her, "Robert is coming back from his vacation and he is trying to get here but it will be about midnight before he can get here, and it is 6 P.M. right now."

"Robert, Robert...I want to talk to Robert," Ann moaned."

Hiding the frustration in his voice, James responded, "I just talked to Robert on the phone, and he won't be here for about six hours!" After this comment, Ann began her final journey...a state of unconsciousness followed by being cognizant for a spell...a roller-coaster where James was relegated to watching Ann float between consciousness and unconsciousness.

James glanced at the clock, noticing it was about 8 P.M. as Ann finally passed her consciousness through the top of her head, which made her transition out of her body more auspicious for her. Both Ann and James knew this was the best way to transit into the higher dimensions of Heaven. And so, it was for Ann, home again, reunited with her Angel friends!

James beseeched the highest of all the powers he knew. "Let this not be the sad end to a story. Let there be more!" James had just suffered the greatest loss in his life—the most important person in his life...his teacher, lover, best friend, confidant and personal Angel. Yet the highest of all powers heard his plea; the amazing Angel, Ann, continues in her loving, indomitable way to advise James about how to smooth his "rough edges," how to share compassion, tolerance, wisdom and love with other people, oh, and to add a layer of insight into Earthly and cosmic events.

This most wise Angel clearly conveyed to James she is here to share her Angelic presence with more than just him. In fact, she indicated very clearly to James she was very disappointed when her sister did not take the T-shirt she

116

wore, which James gave to her, telling him it would very easy for her to contact Ann, when wearing the T-shirt or jewelry which she wore. Additionally, he "heard" how astonished she was at how little her friend, Mindy, bothered to communicate with her, especially since she had a developed ability to do so!

James completely understood her frustrations and concerns, having personally known how much the Angelic Ann can share and guide those in need. Thus, a picture of Ann at the end of this book, with the intention to inspire those who wish to contact her to easily do so. Ann's directive— chant, "Angelic Ann reveal thyself," repeatedly, and she will most likely manifest her presence in your life. You might not see her manifest as a spirit, but you will definitely feel her presence. Ann's prevailing message? *Do not be afraid, Angels are here to help and guide you. Our perspective from the higher dimension which we inhabit is more holistic and complete than anything you can muster in the third dimension on Earth! You are blind compared to Angels.*

James will always feel that the magnificence of the Angelic Ann was virtually ignored while she was here on Earth is rather tragic. Yet if people now will avail themselves of her counsel, then her presence will not have been wasted!

This story comes to an end, as James diligently shares his beloved Ann's insight: *Be aware! There are other Angels like myself who have sacrificed their own comfort, and have incarnated in human bodies on Earth, just as I did.* She further counsels, *"There are many more Angels here than most people would suspect. While many people are focused on the extra-terrestrials that live and work among us, don't forget the Angels. While there are ET's here working to uplift humanity, so are the Angels! Ask and you will be blessed with their presence! Their mandate is to help you, as per Hey Zayin Yod... invoking the presence of Angels! Try it... you'll like it!*

About the Author

Dr. Robert J. Norton has lived much of his life in the way he writes… with a quest to surround himself with the highest level of knowledge in the myriad areas that ensure we live rich, full lives. His education has been extensive, ranging from Speech and English at Cal State Fullerton, to a Juris Doctorate from American College of Law, and many certifications in alternative healing. He formalized his career in Naturopathic Medicine as a graduate of Clayton School of Natural Healing.

Newton has lived to serve others… operating as an award-winning landscape and design company for many years; as a

Christian Science healer to two decades, and more recently… as an author, speaker and life and relationship coach.

Yoga, Metaphysics, Spiritual Sciences, Natural Healing, World Religions, ancient Hermetic teachings—this philosopher and champion for the world has tapped into the roots of spirituality, sexuality, life and love… all with the purpose to enlighten those with a common desire to utilize multiple methods and strategies to approach life more effectively, creatively, radiantly, and with great abundance.

Today, Dr. Newton lives his life looking forward… honoring the love and the beliefs he shared with his wife—and writing more novels to plant a "what if" seed in the minds of his avid readers.

Dr. Newton continues to provide a series of classes and book signings around North and South America, teaching and initiating people into the very practices that lead to immortality.

Please feel free to contact Dr. Newton at:

www.drrobertnewton.com

Theta4ia@yahoo.com for more specifics on his various events. You can also stay connected with him on the following social media platforms.

Amazon Author Central:
https://www.amazon.com/Dr.-Robert-J.-Newton/e/B00LR6A402
Author Website:
http://www.robertjnewtonauthor.com
Website:
www.drrobertnewton.com
Twitter:
https://twitter.com/DrRobertNewton

Goodreads:
https://www.goodreads.com/author/show/18159569.Dr_Robert_Newton

Facebook:
https://www.facebook.com/robert.newton3

https://www.facebook.com/anAngel.not perceived

More Books by This Author

Follow this prolific writer at Amazon Author` Central (Paperback and Print Versions)
https://www.amazon.com/default/e/B00LR6A402

1) **A Map to Healing and Your Essential Divinity Through Theta Consciousness: The Physics of the Immortal "Light Body" and the Creator's Template of Perfection and Abundance for His People (2012)**

   https://www.amazon.com/Healing-Essential-Divinity-Through-Consciousness-ebook/dp/B0792WXKKT

2) **Pathways to God: Experiencing the Energies of the Living God in Your Everyday Life (2012)**

   https://www.amazon.com/Pathways-God-Experiencing-Energies-Everyday-ebook/dp/B0792X14SS

3) **The Hidden Codes of God: A Journey to the Unknown Secrets and Dimensions of the Divine and the Energy of Love (2015)**

https://www.amazon.com/Hidden-Codes-God-Journey-Dimensions-ebook/dp/B00VA0TZ9G

4) **Beyond the Mists of Time: When Trees Ruled the Earth and The State of Balance and Euphoria That Ensued There From (2015)**

https://www.amazon.com/Beyond-Mists-Time-Balance-Euphoria-ebook/dp/B00VAN8L8Y

5) **In Search of the Body Immortal: Let the Journey Begin (2015)**

https://www.amazon.com/Search-Body-Immortal-Journey-Begin-ebook/dp/B016LGBUW8

6) **Planet of the Stupids: Bringing Back the Light of God to Planet Earth—With a Paradise Found (2016)**

https://www.amazon.com/Planet-Stupids-Bringing-Earth-Paradise-ebook/dp/B01DL1MKH0

7) **The Immortality Prophecy: Let the Reveal Begin! (2016)**

https://www.amazon.com/Immortality-Prophecy-Let-Reveal-Begin-ebook/dp/B01IRS689I

8) **A Nation of Deceit: A Nation Deceived ~ A Nation Aggrieved Finding A Solution ~ A New Evolution! (2016)**

https://www.amazon.com/ANationofDeceit-ANation Deceived-Aggrieved-Evolution-ebook/dp/B01MG1NBJ

9) **In Search of the Hidden Codes of God in the Mathematics of Gematria: Discovering the True Da Vinci Code**

https://www.amazon.com/Search-Hidden-Codes-Mathematics-Gematria/dp/0996137165/

An Angel Not Perceived
Dr. Robert J. Newton

An Angel Not Perceived

Dr. Robert J. Newton

www.ingramcontent.com/pod-product-compliance
Lightning Source LLC
Chambersburg PA
CBHW071349170626
46811CB00003B/1052